A Rare Find

We'd worked for over an hour, jabbing and overturning earth with broken tree limbs and scraping dirt with our bare—and now filthy—hands and nails. We'd managed to expose several feet of the silver stuff. It was all bumps (like the one Nina had tripped over) and curlicued lines which were etched into the metal.

"I don't know about that," she said as she slowly traced one of the lines with her fingers. "It's strange; the smooth parts of the metal are freezing cold, but these lines are warm, almost hot in some places. And I think I can hear a soft buzzing sound."

I listened, but I didn't hear anything, and I told Nina so. She shrugged. "Like I said, it's real soft." She stood, but she didn't take her eyes off the thing we'd found.

"You know what, Austin? I think we've found a UFO."

Other Avon books
Compiled and Edited by
Bruce Coville

BRUCE COVILLE'S ALIEN VISITORS
BRUCE COVILLE'S SHAPESHIFTERS
BRUCE COVILLE'S STRANGE WORLDS

BRUCE COVILLE'S UFOs

COMPILED AND EDITED BY
BRUCE COVILLE

ASSISTED BY STEVE ROMAN

Illustrated by Ernie Colón and John Nyberg

A GLC BOOK

Bruce Coville's UFOs

Illustrations by Ernie Colón and John Nyberg.
Interior design by Chris Grassi

Library of Congress Catalog Card Number: 99-96357
ISBN: 0-380-80257-0

First Avon edition, 2000

AVON TRADEMARK REG. U.S. PAT. OFF. AND IN OTHER COUNTRIES, MARCA REGISTRADA, HECHO EN U.S.A.

Contents

INTRODUCTION:

The Invitation

Whenever I am out at night and see a bit of light moving across the sky, my heart leaps with the hope that it might be a UFO.

I'm confident that I am not alone in this reaction. Ever since that mysterious crash in Roswell back in 1949, we Americans have had a kind of UFO-mania—a deep and abiding obsession with the idea that mysterious vehicles from outer space are visiting us on a regular basis.

Just what is it about this idea of "flying saucers" that so intrigues, delights, and compels us?

As you may have suspected, I have a theory. I believe our interest springs from a combination of terror and desire.

The terror is easy enough to understand. If we *are* being monitored by beings from another planet, they must be vastly ahead of us in their scientific knowledge. But are they aggressive, or peaceful? Are they monitoring us as possible friends—or to make us slaves? (Or, as some would have it, simply considering us as a source of food . . .)

As for the desire—well, the more we understand how vast the universe is, the lonelier it feels to think we're the only intelligent creatures in it. (It's also incredibly arrogant to try to cling to that idea, but that's another matter altogether.) If we are being visited by aliens, it proves that we're not alone.

Sharpening that desire is the strange but indisputable fact that the human heart loves mystery. And in a world that has been so fully explored and mapped and charted that we are quickly running out of unknown corners, UFOs represent a truly compelling mystery, facing us with such questions as:

What kind of creatures made those vehicles?

Why are they watching us?

What do they want?

And—perhaps most frightening of all when we really

consider it—*what do they think of us?*

In the stories that follow, thirteen talented and highly creative (not to mention deeply weird) writers try to imagine the answers to these questions. As so often happens, the variety of their responses is greater than I could have guessed when we began gathering this collection, with settings that range from ancient Egypt to distant planets, and ideas that draw equally from the wells of horror, humor, and hope.

But then every UFO sighting, real or imagined, carries with it the hopeful fear and the fearful hope that we might be on the verge of making contact with an alien civilization. And in the end, I think that's why UFOs are so exciting. These are not only the vehicles by which the aliens will reach us; they are, if all goes well, the vehicles that will take us to the stars.

But consider this: perhaps the purpose of the makers of these flying saucers is more subtle. What if their real goal is to inspire us to make the journey ourselves?

In the sports world, there is a well-known phenomenon whereby an achievement people think is impossible—such as the four-minute mile—may stand for years, or even decades. Yet as soon as one person breaks this "impossible" barrier, many others begin to repeat the achievement. What has changed? Not their skill. Not their strength. Not their bodies.

What has changed is their sense of possibility.

So perhaps the greatest thing about flying saucers is that they tell us it's possible to escape our planetary bonds and explore the universe.

Maybe our mysterious visitors never intend to make contact while we're still planetbound.

Maybe what they're offering is an invitation to join them in the greater galaxy—an invitation that comes not by showing us how it's done, but simply by showing us it's possible.

The rest is up to us.

The stars are waiting.

Isn't it time we got busy?

Bruce Coville

Shadow of the Pyramid

by Noreen Doyle

During the reign of my brother the king, Khufu, Lord of the Two Lands, the Gray-Men came to Egypt.

The Nile was about to flood as it does every year. In this season, while the high waters are laying rich new soil across the fields, farmers can neither sow nor plow. So the king called north to the marshes of the Delta and south to the hills of Nubia.

"You cannot work your fields today, for the Nile will flood them tomorrow," he said. "Come to me, for I have work for you. I will feed you and I will clothe you. Come labor for me and if you die here I will give you a burial finer than you would ever receive in your little villages. Come work for me!"

His summons was heard; it was obeyed. The governors of the provinces assembled men of strength and skill and care and sent them forth. As the Nile inundated the fields, a flood of people came by boat and bare foot to the region of Memphis.

We saw lights in the sky during those days. Our priests know the sky well and declared that these were not the lights that fall to earth from time to time in the form of black stones. No, these were like slender, bright fish that swam in the heavens, and never once did one fall.

"Are they gods?" the king asked of the priests. The

priests did not know. Wise men from foreign lands assembled before the throne, speaking in strange tongues and smelling of strange perfumes. From Syria and Sumer and beyond Nubia they came, but they did not know. Magicians spoke to ghosts in bowls of oiled waters, and *they* did not know.

"Should these omens delay construction of my tomb?" Khufu asked of his ministers.

Now, these ministers did not want to delay construction of the pyramid. The royal tomb was their purpose and their power. I know this to be true, for I, Kanefer, the king's royal brother, am foremost of his ministers.

"No," I said. "Let us not delay construction of your tomb, my lord. Twenty thousand men sit along the riverbank, awaiting royal orders. Quarries are pregnant with stone. Let us raise a monument to your majesty, that these fish in the sky will see your might and be afraid!"

Upon his order we began construction of his great pyramid.

With tools of copper, wood, and stone, quarrymen broke limestone from the hills. In wooden barges, sailors shipped them down the swollen river. On sledges of wood, along tracks slicked with water, laborers dragged the blocks into place with ropes. One course, two courses, three courses of stone, it rose, year after year. The king's pyramid, his house of eternity, grew toward heaven.

Still the fish flashed in the sky at night, at dusk, at dawn, at midday. Although afraid, the laborers knew that their king would protect them; after all, did not archers and spearsmen stand ready? Because Khufu gave them food and shelter and promise of the sweet afterlife, because he was their king, the workmen did not let the fish in the sky devour their courage.

Each year when the Nile receded and the fields lay ready for planting, most of the workmen went home again to their farms. Many craftsmen stayed behind, for there was always work to be done. Nevertheless, during these seasons it was easier to be alone at the pyramid. After the clamoring of laborers ("More rope!" "More bread!") and the nattering of my fellow ministers ("Is there enough gold in the treasury?" "What if there is nothing good for dinner tonight?"), I often longed to escape the company of others.

So one evening I walked, alone, and stood, alone, on the rising majesty of the royal tomb. The fish flashed in the sky. I had almost ceased to notice them anymore, but one of them hung over my head. I could see its belly and knew that it was no fish. It had no fins, its tail was pointed like its head, and its lights were set into skin blacker than the kohl I paint around my eyes.

This fish descended from the sky until it hung twenty cubits above the unfinished pyramid. Like a statue I stood there beneath its belly; my arms were no longer mine, and I could not call my legs my own.

A hole opened in the belly of this fish and from this burst forth light that blinded me like the rising sun. I was borne into the air, certain that it meant to devour me. Ah, but this hole was no mouth. It was a door.

This was not a fish, I thought, but a boat! I found myself in a cabin of unrivaled whiteness, with walls as smooth as an alabaster bowl. Through one of these walls walked a creature dressed in silver cloth. It was the size and shape of a man but as hairless as a babe. It was big of head and eye, thin of arm and lip. Its skin had the color of ash.

The Gray-Man laid me upon a cold table. Having stripped from me kilt and cloak and all my jewelry, with cold instruments it prodded me at front and at back, it poked me at top and at bottom.

I wished to cry (yes, even like a child) for the pain was so great. But I could move no more than could a corpse on the embalmer's table. O, but I was no corpse. My *ka*-soul and my *ba*-soul still dwelt within my breast. Would the Gray-Man trap them in this body? Would I be unable to enter the Blessed Fields of the afterlife? I feared being trapped in whiteness for a million years.

Then I became aware of nothing, for which to this very day I give thanks to every god.

When I awoke, my kilt and cloak and jewelry were laid on a table and I was alone. I dressed. The Gray-Man had stolen nothing of mine, not so much as one gold ring.

Again it walked through a wall to stand beside me. It showed me a window through which I could see its country.

From workshops without craftsmen came garments of silver threads and tiny loaves of bread which they ate. (And they ate nothing else; not so much as an onion, not one lettuce leaf!) Each Gray-Man had its garment and its bread and indeed its everything delivered by strange servants. Some were sky-boats. Others were sledges or statues brought to life by magic. All appeared to be made of copper, silver, or gold; they flew through the air or moved along the ground, wingless, footless, and noiseless.

If only Egypt had these things! I thought. Dare I, brother of the king of Egypt so rich in gold, ask the Gray-Man for such servants?

Before I could ponder this further, my heart seemed to speak to me! But it was not my heart. It was the Gray-Man who spoke, without words, without any sound.

A hundred thousand years ago, our ancestors bestowed upon us these wonderful things. Things-that-think determine what we need. Things-small-beyond-sight create what we need. Things-that-bring give us what we need. But now our things have grown old and slow. We need more than the things-that-think will think of, more than the things-small-beyond-sight will make, more than the things-that-bring will give. Someday, none of them will think or make or bring at all. So we travel. So we think. I have thought about you.

"You have," I agreed. I hoped that it had finished "thinking" about me with its cold instruments. "Why have you thought about me? Why do you fly through the skies above us, doing nothing more?"

We seek answers. But my examination of you has not provided answers. I must have answers.

The Gray-Men were not gods, I realized. This emboldened me.

I decided that in return for my answers to its questions, it would answer questions of mine. Egypt would know the secret of these sky-boats, of these sledges and statues that moved by themselves. In a single year we could build a pyramid and raise mighty fortresses along our frontiers. We could travel the earth and bring home the riches of every foreign land. No more would our sailors be at the mercy of the sea. No more would our caravans be at the mercy of the desert. Egypt would rule the sky.

But in the end I never asked, and I was returned home with only the story that you now read. The Gray-Men do not know the answers to my questions. Although they have the things of their ancestors, they do not have the *knowledge* of their ancestors. The Gray-Men live by the dictates of the things-that-think, and are parasites on the produce of the things-small-beyond-sight given to them by the things-that-bring. How these things work, and how their ancestors made them, are as much a mystery to the Gray-Men as they are to me.

And I learned this when the Gray-Man showed me through its window my own country: in the shadow of the pyramid, Egyptians hauled stone blocks up an earthen ramp; sweat slicked the ground at their feet, and ropes made bruises upon their backs; and they sang joyously to keep the rhythm of their labor.

The question the Gray-Man asked of me was this: "Will you teach us how to build?"

A Lot of Saucers

by Harlan Ellison

It wasn't just one sighting, or a covey, or a hundred. It was five thousand. Exactly five thousand of them, and all at the same time. They appeared in the skies over Earth instantaneously.

One instant the sky was empty and grey and flecked with cloud formations . . . the next they blotted out the clouds, and cast huge, elliptical shadows along the ground.

They were miles in diameter, and perfectly round, and there was no questioning—even for an incredulous second—that they were from outer space somewhere. They hung a mile above the Earth, over the 30th parallel. Over Los Angeles and the Sahara Desert and Baghdad and the Canary Islands and over Shanghai. There was no great empty space left between them, for they girdled the Earth with a band of discs. Where everyone could see them, so no one could doubt their power or their menace.

Yet they hung silently. As though waiting.

Waiting.

"The perplexing thing about it, General, is that every once in a while, one of them just goes *flick!* and disappears. In a little while another one *flicks!* and takes its place. Not the same one, either, We can tell. There are different markings on them. Nobody can figure it out."

Alberts was a Captain, properly deferential to the Commanding General. He was short, but dapper; clothes hung well on him; hair thinning across his skull; eyes alert, and a weariness in the softness and line of his body: a man who had been too long in grade, too long as Captain, with Colonel's rank out of reach. He folded his hands across his paunch, finished his speech, and settled back in the chair.

He stared across the desk at the General. The General steepled his blocky fingers, rocked back and forth in the big leather chair. He stared at his Adjutant with a veiled expression. Adjutant: the politically correct word for assistant, second-in-charge, gopher, the guy who actually got the job done. The General had found Alberts when he was a Second Looey, and knew he had a treasure when Alberts solved ten thorny problems in two days. He wasn't about to upgrade this Captain . . . he needed him right there, serving the General's needs. Adjutant: it sounded better than slave.

"How long—to the hour—have they been here now, Captain?" His tone was almost chiding, definitely aggressive.

He waited silently for an answer as the Adjutant leafed through a folder, consulted his watch, and closed his eyes in figuring. Finally the Adjutant leaned forward and said, "Three days, eight and one-half hours, General."

"And nothing has been done about them yet," the heavy-faced Air Force man replied. It was not a question; it was a statement, and one that demanded either an explanation or an alibi.

The Adjutant knew he had no explanation, so he offered the alibi. "But, General, what *can* we do? We don't dare scramble a flight of interceptors. Those things are almost four miles around, and there's no telling what they'd do if we made a hostile move . . . or even a move that *looked* hostile.

"We don't know where they come from or what they want. Or what's inside them. But if they were smart enough to *get* here, they're surely smart enough to stop any offensive action we might take. We're stuck, General. Our hands are tied."

The General leaned forward, and his sharp blue eyes caught the Adjutant's face in a vise-lock stare. "Captain, don't you *ever* use that word around me. The first thing I learned, when I was a plebe at West Point, was that the hands of the United States Air Force are *never* tied. You understand that?"

The Captain shifted uneasily, made an accepting motion with his hand. "Yes, but, General . . . what . . ."

"I said *never,* Captain Alberts! And by that I mean you'd better get out there and do something, right now."

The Adjutant rose hastily to his feet, slid the chair back an inch, and saluted briskly. Turning on his heel, he left the office, a frozen frown on his face. For the first time since he'd gotten this cushy job with the General, it looked as though there was going to be work involved. Worse, it might be danger.

Captain Harold Alberts, Adjutant, was terribly frightened, for the first time since he'd been appointed to the General's staff.

* * *

The saucers seemed to be holding a tight formation. They hovered, and lowered not an inch. They were separated by a half mile of empty space on either side, but were easily close enough to pick off anyone flying between them . . . should that be their intent.

They were huge things, without conning bubbles or landing gear, without any visible projections of any sort. Their skins were of some non-reflective metal, for it could be seen that the sun was glinting on them, yet was casting off no burst of radiance. It made the possibility that this was some super-strong metal, seem even more possible. They were silent behemoths, around which the air lanes of the world had had to be shifted. They did not move, nor did they show evidence of life. They were two cymbals, laid dead face-on-face.

They were simply *there,* and what sort of contesting could there be to that?

Every few hours, at irregular intervals (with no pattern that could be clocked or computed) one of the ships would disappear. Over the wasted sands of the Sahara, or above the crowded streets of Shanghai, or high over the neon of Las Vegas, one of the ships would waver for an instant, as though being washed by some invisible wave, then *flick!* and it would be gone. And in that moment the sun would stream through, covering the area that had been shadowed by the elliptical darkness. Shortly thereafter—but only sometimes shortly; occasionally a full hour or two would elapse—another ship would appear in the vanished one's spot. It would not be the same ship, because the one that had disappeared might have been ringed with blue lines, while this new one had a large green dot at its top-center.

But there it was, right in place, a half mile away from each neighbor on either side, and casting that fearful shadow along the ground.

Storm clouds formed above them, and spilled their contents down. The rain washed across their smooth, metallic tops, and ran off, to soak the ground a mile beneath.

They made no move, and they offered no hostility, but—as the hardware dealer in San Francisco said—"My God, the things could *blast* us at any second!" And—as the Berber tribesman, talking to his dromedary-mounted fellows said—"Even if they hang silent, they come from *somewhere,* and I'm frightened, terribly frightened."

So it went, for a week, with the terror clogging the throats of Earthmen around the world. This was not some disaster that happened in Mississippi, so the people of Connecticut could read about it and shake their heads, then worry no more. This was something that affected everyone, and a great segment of the Earth's population *lived* under those sleek metal vehicles from some far star.

This was terror incarnate.

Getting worse with each passing day.

The Adjutant felt his career frustration, his deep anger, his distaste for this pompous piss-ant of a General growing rapidly. He had worked as the General's aide for three years now, and been quite happy with the assignment. The General was an important man, and it was therefore surprising how few actual top-rung decisions had to be made by him, without first being checked and double-checked by underlings.

The Captain knew his General thought he was a pride-and-joy. Certainly he did; the Adjutant made most of the decisions, and all the General had to do was hand out the orders. Without ever letting the General know his work was being done for him by an aide, the Adjutant had become indispensable. "A good man, that Alberts," the General said, at the Officers' Club.

But this crisis with the saucers was something else. It had been dumped in the General's lap, both from above, and from below, and he was sweating. He had to solve this problem, and for the first time in his life his rough-hewn good looks and military bearing and good name could not bluff him through.

He actually had to make a meaningful decision, and he was almost incapable of doing it. That made him edgy, and snappish, and dissatisfied, and it made the Adjutant's job not quite so cushy.

"Confound it, Alberts! This isn't some base maneuver you can stammer through! This is a nationwide emergency, and everyone is on my neck! God knows I'm doing all I can, but I need a little help! I've tried to impress upon you the—the—*seriousness* of the matter; this thing has got to be ended. It's got the world in an uproar. You're getting up my nose with this attitude, boy! It's starting to stink like subordination, Alberts . . ."

The Adjutant watched, his mouth a fine line. This was the first time the General had spoken to him with such demeaning manner. He didn't like it, a lot, but it was just another sign of the cracking facade of the old man.

The General had come from wealthy Army parents, been sent through West Point and graduated with top honors. He had joined the Air Force when the Army and Air Corps were one and the same, and stayed on after the separation. He had served in the air, and risen in the ranks almost faster than the eye could see. Mostly through his father's connections. The honors, the service duty, the medals . . . all through pull.

The man was a wealthy, sheltered, and vacillating individual, and the Adjutant had been making his decisions for three years. Alberts wondered what would happen when the rotation plan moved him to another job, next year. Would the new Adjutant catch on as fast as he had from the last one? Or would the General pull strings so he could stay on?

But that was all in the future, and this saucer decision was one the General had to make for himself. It wasn't minor.

And the General was cracking. Badly.

"Now get up there and *do* something!" the General cried, slamming the empty desktop with a flattened hand.

His face was blotched with frustration and annoyance, and—naturally—Alberts saluted, swiveled, and left.

Thinking, *I hope the Pentagon lowers the boom right down his wattled throat, right down his gullet to his large colon!*

One saucer was a dirty affair. Not with the dust and filth of an atmosphere, for the saucer had obviously not been very long in air, but with the pocks and blazes of space. Here a small cluster of pits, where the saucer had encountered a meteor swarm; there a bright smear of oxidized metal. Its markings were slovenly, and there were obvious patchings on its metal hull.

Somehow, it seemed out of place among all the bright, shining, marvelously-intricate painted saucers. It seemed to be a rather poor relation, and never, *never* flickered out of existence. All the others might be subject to that strange disappearing act, but not the poor relation. It stayed where it was, somewhere above the Fairchild Desert of Nevada.

Once a civilian pilot from Las Vegas, disregarding the orders of the C.A.P., flew very close to the dirty saucer. The pilot buzzed the ship several times, swooping in and over and back around in huge, swinging arcs. By the time he had made his fourteenth Immelmann and decided to land atop the saucer, just for yuks, the hurry-up bleep was out to interceptors based near Reno and Winnemucca, and they caught him high, blasting him from the sky in a matter of minutes.

With the fate of a world hanging in the balance, there could be no time for subtlety or reasoning with crackpots. He had been irrational, had defied the stay-grounded, keep-back orders, and so had fallen under the martial law which had ruled the country since the day after the five thousand had appeared.

Radio communication with the ships was impossibly fruitless.

Television transmission was equally worthless.

Bounced signals failed to come back; the metal of the ships sopped them up.

Telemetering devices brought back readings of the density—or *seeming* density—of the ships, and when they were reported, the situation looked bleaker than before.

The metal was, indeed, super-strong.

The only time things looked promising was when a philologist and a linguist were recruited to broadcast a complete course in English for thirty-six hours straight. The beam was directed at first one ship, then another, and finally when it was directed at the dirty saucer, was gulped in.

They continued broadcasting, till at the end of thirty-six hours, the dumpy, red-faced, runny-nosed, and sniffling Linguist, who had picked up his cold in the broadcasting shack, pushed back his chair, gathered his cashmere sweater from where it had fallen in the corner, and said there was no use.

No reply had come in. If the beings who had flown these saucers were intelligent enough to have gotten here, they would surely have been intelligent enough to have learned English by then. But there had been no reply, and spirits sank again.

Inter-channel memos slipped frantically down from President to Aide, to Secretary of Defense, to Undersecretary, to Chief of Staff, to the General, who passed the memos—bundled—to his Adjutant. Who worried.

It had been the only one where there was any slightest sign of contact. "Look, pilot, I want you to fly across that dirty one," the Adjutant said.

"Begging the Captain's permission . . ." the wide-eyed young pilot demanded, over his shoulder; he continued at the nod from Alberts. ". . . but the last man who buzzed that big-O, sir, got himself scissored good and proper. What I mean, sir, is that we're way off bounds, and if our clearances didn't, uh, clear, we might have a flock of my buddies down our necks." He spoke in a faint Texas drawl that seemed to ease from between his thin lips.

The Adjutant felt the adrenaline flowing erratically. He had been taking slop from the General for three weeks, and now to be forced into flying up himself, into the very jaws of death (as he phrased it to himself), to look over the situation . . . he would brook no backtalk from a whey-faced flight boy fresh out of Floyd Bennett.

Alberts shooed him off, directed him back to the stick. "Don't worry yourself, pilot." He licked his lips, added, "They cleared, and all we have to worry about is that saucer line up ahead."

The discs were rising out of the late evening Nevada haze. The clouds seemed to have lowered, and the fog seemed to have risen, and the two intermingled, giving a wavering, indistinct appearance to the metallic line of saucers, stretching off beyond the horizon.

The Adjutant looked out through the curving bubble of the helicopter's control country, and felt the same twinges of fear rippling the hair along his neck that he had felt when the General had started putting the screws to him.

The Sikorsky rescue copter windmilled in toward the saucer, its rotors *flap-flap-flap-flapping* overhead.

The pilot sticked-in on the dirty saucer. It rose out of the mist abruptly, and they were close enough to see that there really *was* dust streaked with dirt along the dull metal surface of the ship. *Probably from one of these Nevada windstorms,* the Adjutant thought.

They scaled down, and came to a hovering stop two feet above the empty metal face of the disc.

"See anything?" the Adjutant asked.

The pilot craned off to one side, swept his gaze around, then turned on the searchbeam. The pole of light watered across the sleek saucer bulk, and picked up nothing. Not even a line of rivets, not even a break in the construction. Nothing but dirt and pockmarks, and what might be considered patches, were this a tire or an ordinary ship.

"Nothing, sir."

"Take us over there, right there, will you, pilot?"

The Adjutant indicated a lighter place on the metal of the ship. It seemed to be a different shade of chrome-color. The Sikorsky jerked, lifted a few inches, and slid over. The pilot brought it back down, and they looked over the hull of the saucer at that point.

It was, indeed, lighter in shade.

"This *could* be something, pi—"

The shaft rose up directly in front of the Sikorsky before he could finish the word.

It was a column of transparent, almost glass-like material, with a metal disc sealing off the top. It was rising out of the metal where there had been no break in the skin, and it kept rising till it towered over them.

"M-m-m—" the Adjutant struggled to get the word loose.

"Move!" he finally spat out, but before they could whip away, the *person* stepped up inside the column, stared straight out, his gigantic face on a line with their cab.

He must have been thirty feet tall, and completely covered with reddish-brown hair. His ears were pointed, and set almost atop his head. The eyes were pocketed by deep ridges of matted hair, and his nose was a pair of breather-slits. His hands hung far below his indrawn waist, and they were eight-fingered. Each finger was a tentacle that writhed with a separate life of its own. He wore a loose-fitting and wrinkled, dirty sort of toga affair, patched and covered with stains.

He stared at them unblinking. For he had no eyelids.

"Gawd Almighty!" the pilot squawked, and fumbled blindly at his controls for an instant, unable to tear his eyes away from the being before them. Finally his hand met the controls, and the Sikorsky bucked backward, tipped, and rose rapidly above the saucer, spiraling away into the night as fast as the rotors would windmill. In a minute the copter was gone.

The glassite pillar atop the dirty saucer remained raised for a few minutes, then slowly sank back into the ship.

No mark was left where it had risen out.

Somehow, news of the *person* leaked out. And from then on, telescopes across the world were trained on the unbroken band of discs circling the Earth. They watched in shifts, not wanting to miss a thing, but there was nothing more to see. No further contact was made, in person or by radio.

There was no sign of life anywhere along the chain of discs. They could have been empty for all anyone knew. Going into the eighth week, no one knew any more about them than on the day they had arrived.

No government would venture an exploratory party, for the slightest hint of a wrong move or word might turn the unleashed wrath of the saucers on the Earth.

Stocks fell quickly and crazily. Shipping was slowed to a standstill, and production fell off terrifically in factories. No one wanted to work when they might be blown up at any moment. People began a disorganized exodus to the hills and swamps and lost places of the planet. If the saucers were going to wash the cities with fire and death, no one wanted to be there when it happened.

They were not hostile, and that was what kept the world moving in its cultural tracks; but they were *alien*, they were from the *stars!* And that made them objects of terror.

Tempers were short; memos had long since been replaced by curses and demands. Allegations were thrown back and forth across the oceans. Dereliction of duty proceedings were begun on dozens of persons in high places.

The situation was worsening every moment. In the tenth week the nasty remarks ceased, and there were rumors of a court-martial. And a firing squad.

"Got to *do* something, Alberts. Got to do *some*thing!"

The Adjutant watched the spectacle of his superior shattering with something akin to sorrow. There went the cushy job.

"But what, General?" He kept his voice low and modulated. No sense sending the old boy into another tantrum.

"I—I want to go up there . . . see what he looks like . . . see what I can d-do . . ."

An hour later the Sikorsky carried the General to the Maginot Line of silent saucers.

Twenty minutes later he was back, bathed in sweat, and white as a fish-belly. "Horrible. All hair and eyes. Horrible. Horrible." He croaked a few more words, and sank into a chair.

"Call Ordnance," he breathed gaspingly. "Prepare a missile.

"With an atomic warhead.

"Now!"

They attached the parasite missile beneath a night-fighter, checking and double-checking the release mechanism.

Before they released the ship, they waited for the General's okay. This wasn't just a test flight, this was an atomic missile, and whatever the repercussions, they wanted them on the General's head, not their own.

In the base office, the Adjutant was replacing the phone in its cradle. "What did Washington say, General?" he asked the trembling officer.

"They said the situation was in my hands. I was free to do as I saw fit. The President can't be located. They think he's been smuggled with his cabinet, out West somewhere, to the mountains."

The General did not look at his Adjutant as he spoke the words. He stared at his clasped and shaking hands.

"Tell them to release the missile. We'll watch it on TV."

The Adjutant lifted the phone, clicked the connection buttons twice, spoke quickly, softly, into the mouth-piece. "Let it go."

A minute and a half later, from half a mile away on the launching strip, they heard the jet revv-up and split the evening sky with its fire.

Then they went to the television room and watched the lines of screens.

In one they saw the silent girdle of saucers. In another they were focused on the dirty saucer, with a sign above the screen that said INITIAL TARGET. In a third they had a line-of-sight to the night-fighter's approach pattern.

"There it comes!" one of the technicians yelled, pointing at the lighter dark of the jet as it streaked toward the massed saucers, leaving a trail of fire behind it.

They watched silently as the plane swooped in high, dove, and they saw the parasite leave its belly, streak on forward. The jet sliced upward, did a roll, and was a mile away as the parasite homed in exactly.

They watched with held breath as the small atomic missile deaded-in on the dirty saucer, and they flinched as it struck.

A blinding flash covered all the screens for a moment, and a few seconds later they heard the explosion. Shock waves ripped outward and the concussion was great enough to knock out eighteen of the thirty telemetering cameras.

But they could see the dirty saucer clearly on one. In that one the smoke and blast were clearing slowly. A mushroom-shaped cloud was rising, rising, rising from the sloping dish of the saucer's upper side. As it moved away they could see oxidized smears and blast pattern of white jagged sunbursts. It looked as harmless as a kid's experiment with a match, potassium nitrate, and powdered magnesium. It had not harmed the saucer in the least. But . . .

There was a crack along the top face of the saucer. And from that gash spilled a bubbling white substance. The stuff frothed out and ran across the top of the saucer. It pitted and tore at the metal of the ship wherever it touched. There was a weird sound of clacking and coughing from the ship, as though some intricate mechanism within were erupting.

Then, as they watched, the glassite pillar rose up out of the ship . . .

. . . and the *person* was within.

Unmistakably, his face was a violence of rage and hatred. His fists beat against the glassite, and he roared—silently, for no sound could be picked up by the audio ears—inside the pillar. He spat, and blood—red and thick—dotted the clear glassite. His mouth opened screaming wide and long, sharp teeth could be seen.

He shook a fist at the emptiness beyond the saucer, and the pillar lowered into the ship.

A minute later, for the first time since it had arrived, the dirty saucer *flicked!* out of existence and was gone.

"That was perhaps the wrong move, General . . ."

The General, who had been fastened to the TV screen by some invisible linkage, tore his eyes away from the set, and whirled, glowering, on his Adjutant.

"That's for *me* to worry about, Captain Alberts. I told you the military mind can solve problems by the direct method, the uncomplicated method, while these scientists dawdle and doodle helplessly." He was speaking loudly, almost hysterically, and the Adjutant recognized relief in the officer's tones.

"They're on the run!" the General shouted, grinning hugely. "On the run, by George! Now, come on, Alberts, let's get a few antiaircraft battalions out there on the desert and pick off the rest of them in this area. Wait till the President hears of *this!*"

They were out on the desert, the ack-ack guns sniffing at the sky, pelting the saucers from six separate batteries.

They were intent on what they were doing, certain that anyone in those other ships

(and why did the Adjutant keep getting the feeling that those other ships were *empty?*)

would turn tail and disappear as quickly as the dirty saucer had done an hour and a quarter before.

They had just lobbed five fast shells at a snow-white saucer with purple markings, when the dirty saucer reappeared.

Flick!

He was back, that hairy alien in the dirty, stained toga. He was back in the same spot he had vacated, almost directly above the General's batteries.

The pillar rose, and the General watched stunned as the metal top slid off the pillar, and the alien stepped out.

He stepped onto the top of his ship, and they saw the gash in the hull had been repaired. Caulked with some sort of black sticky stuff that stuck to the alien's clawed feet as he walked along the top of the saucer. He carried a thick, gun-like object in his hands, cradled against his massive chest.

Then he screamed something in a voice like thunder. They could hear it only roughly, for it was in a guttural tongue. Then he switched to English, and screamed again, in more detail.

The General strained his ears. His hearing had never been the best, but the Adjutant heard, it was clear to see, from the look of horror and failure and frustration on his face. Then the Adjutant dove away from the antiaircraft gun, rolled over several times, and sprinted out into the desert.

The General hesitated only a moment before following, but that was enough.

The alien turned the gun-like object on the batteries, and a roar and a flash sent the metal screaming skyward, ripping and shredding. Bodies were flung in every direction, and a blue pallor settled across the landscape as a thirty-foot crater opened where the battery had been.

The General felt himself lifted, buffeted, and thrown. He landed face forward in the ditch, and saw his arm land five feet away. He screamed; the pain in his left side was excruciating.

He screamed again, and in a moment Alberts was beside him, dragging him away from the area of destruction. The alien was standing spraddle-legged atop his machine, blasting, blasting, scouring the Earth with blue fire.

The alien screamed in English again, and then he stepped into the pillar, which lowered into the ship once more. A few seconds later the ship *flicked!* away, and materialized in the sky ten miles off, above the air base.

There was more blasting, and the blue pallor lit the sky for a full half hour, then.

The saucer *flicked!* and was gone. A few moments later the blue pallor—fainter yet, but strengthening all the time—was seen twenty miles further on, washing Las Vegas.

Flick! Flick! Flick!

And a dozen more saucers, dirtier than the first, materialized, paused a moment as though getting their bearings, then *flicked!* away.

For the next hours the blue pallor filled the sky, and it was easy to see the scouring was moving across the planet systematically.

The General's head was cradled in his Adjutant's lap. He was sinking so rapidly there was no hope at all. His entire left side had been scorched and ripped open. He lay there, looking up at the face of the once-dapper Adjutant, his eyes barely focusing. His tongue bulged from his mouth, and then a few words.

Haltingly, "I . . . c-couldn't hear . . . what he s-said, Al-b-berts. W-what . . . did . . . he . . . say?"

The General's eyes closed, but his chest still moved. The Adjutant felt all the hatred he had built for this man vanish. Though the blustering fool had caused the death of a world, still he was dying, and there was no sense letting him carry that guilt with him.

"Nothing, General. Nothing at all. You did your very best, sir."

Then he realized the last "sir" had been spoken uselessly. The General was dead.

"You did your best, sir," the Adjutant spoke to the night. "It wasn't your fault the attendant picked us.

"All the alien said was that there were destructive pests in this *parking lot,* and he was one attendant who was going to clear them out even if he had to work overtime for a century."

The words faded in the night, and only the blue pallor remained. Growing, flashing, never waning. Never.

The Toy Room

by David Honigsberg

The room was full of toys.

Toys of all types; toys for older children and younger children. He guessed that there was such a variety because his captors—that's how he thought of them—really had no idea how old he was. They hadn't bothered to try to find out and he certainly didn't want to tell them. He stood in the center of the room and looked at the toys.

As his gaze flicked from one toy to another, he again became aware of the hum. At times he barely noticed it. Other times, it seemed as though it was the loudest sound in the world. He guessed that it was the sound that the engines made, sure that he had been taken prisoner and was now orbiting his world on some kind of spaceship. He wondered why his captors didn't seem to hear it. He thought that it must be because they'd become used to it during all their time in space.

He could figure out how some of the toys and games worked just by looking at them or experimenting a little. Others he couldn't play because they had what must be instructions printed on them. He hadn't yet learned to read their language. Speaking it was difficult enough, although some of the toys had helped him learn a basic vocabulary in a relatively short time. He didn't really want to spend time deciphering the lines and curves of their writing.

He was also quite sure his every move was being watched. How else would they know exactly what time he awoke each day? Within moments, one of them would enter the room he slept in with the odd things that passed for food on their world, wherever it was. At least nothing had made him sick, even if it all tasted bad to him.

More proof of the location of his prison was the window on the toy room's wall. Day in and day out, it showed the same thing. Nothing ever changed. He had tried to open it a few times, but he couldn't. He was sure that it wasn't a window at all, just some kind of lifelike image they thought would make him feel that he wasn't in space. He knew better, though.

He also knew that he was expected to play. He found the game which had quickly become his favorite. It was an odd-looking contraption with very simple controls—a series of colored buttons and a stick that he could hold onto. Attached to the game was a device that had to be placed in front of the player's eyes so that the visual effects could be seen. It had taken him a while to figure out how best to wear it, as his head was a different size from that of the child the game was designed for, but his efforts had been well worth it.

He pressed a button to turn on the game, then pressed others in a combination which brought him the satisfaction of seeing what looked like the control panel of a small spaceship. He had learned how to use the stick to make the little ship turn and move, although he couldn't get used to seeing alien hands in his viewscreen mirroring the movements his own hands made. Other ships appeared on the screen, and he moved the stick and pushed buttons until the ships had all been destroyed.

He knew that there would be a moment before more ships appeared, so he practiced flying the little ship, pretending that he was piloting it home, away from his shipboard prison. In too short a time, though, more ships appeared and he got caught up in his efforts to shoot them down. Even though the game was probably meant for children much younger than himself, he enjoyed it and often played it for long periods of time. Although he sometimes played with other toys, he always came back to that one.

The team leader watched the subject's movements on the main monitor.

"Do you see how easily it handles that game?" he asked his assistant.

"Yes. It's figured it out faster than any of the others," she answered, while making a few entries into her computer. "It's learned to speak our language faster, too."

"Do the medical tests confirm that it's different in any way?"

"Not in the least. There's nothing to explain this whatsoever. It must be smarter. We were lucky this time. We should hold on to it for a while longer."

"That might not be easy. It's been showing classic signs of restlessness. If we don't let it go soon, it might be too much for us to handle."

The assistant glanced at the monitor. The subject had begun to pace back and forth, looking at one toy after another, passing many without a glance, sometimes stopping to examine a select few, but making no additional selections.

"Perhaps I can talk to it and convince it that everything is going to be all right."

The subject stopped in front of a series of wooden blocks. Carefully bending down, it picked one up and threw it as hard as he could, watching as it bounced off the wall with a satisfying *clunk*. It picked up another, and repeated the procedure. Then it picked up a third, a fourth, a fifth, throwing again and again until there were no more blocks left.

"Are you sure you want to do that?" asked the team leader. "It seems much stronger than our children back home. If that's so, you're probably weaker than any female that it's encountered before."

The assistant got up and walked to the door. "It's worth trying, I think. We don't want it tearing the place apart, do we?"

"Definitely not," he responded as his assistant closed the door behind her.

The room was full of toys.

He stood near the wall, watching as it shut the door. He wondered what lay beyond, since his movements were confined to this room and the smaller room in which he slept. It had to step with care so as not to break anything as it approached. He noticed that it was smaller than the ones who brought the food, and he had lost count of the times he had thought that the aliens had eyes and heads that weren't the right size. When it was a few paces from him, it knelt down so it could look at him better.

"Hello," it said, its face contorting into what he had decided was a happy expression. He tried to match it, knowing that it was only an approximation at best, a sad imitation at worst.

"Hello," he answered back, making sure to pronounce the word so that it could understand him.

"Why did you throw those?" it asked, pointing at one of the cubes on the floor.

He didn't answer. If there was any doubt as to whether he was being watched, the question erased it. There was no way it could have known that he had thrown the cubes if it hadn't somehow seen it happen.

"I thought you might be angry," it said.

"Angry?"

"Maybe 'unhappy' is a better word."

He gazed at it, not understanding what it meant.

"Not happy," it said. "'Un' is the same as 'not.'"

"Yes. I am unhappy."

"Can you tell me why?"

"I do un like it here."

It made the happy face again. "You mean you do not like it here."

He stared at it, confused. Their language was very hard to learn. "You said 'un' is 'not,'" he complained.

"Only sometimes. If you stay with us you will learn, though. Do you want to stay?"

He had never thought about staying and knew he didn't want to. "No! I want to go home! I want to see my . . ." He paused. He did not know their word for "parents." He used his own language instead.

He knew it didn't understand. None of them really seemed interested in learning his language. They only gave him what he needed to learn theirs. It nodded anyway.

"We will bring you home soon," it said. "All you have to do is stay a little longer."

"I do not want to stay. I want to go now."

"Yes. I'm sure you do." It stood up and looked down at him. "Soon."

"Soon," he repeated, and tried to make the happy face again.

"Good," it said. "Very good." It walked to the door and left him alone in the room. He collected the wooden cubes and began to throw them again.

"It smiled at you," the team leader said when she returned to the control room. "That might be a good sign."

"Unless it's just imitating me and doesn't really know what a smile means," the assistant answered. She pointed to the monitors, which showed the subject throwing the cubes. "There's no way to tell."

The leader looked thoughtful. "True. Even so, I think it's a step in the right direction. It's certainly more than we've gotten from the others. They haven't shown any interest in communicating with us at all. This one's different. I hope that we don't have to dissect it to figure out why."

"That would be a failure," she said, shuddering at the thought. "I'm growing quite fond of it and would hate to have to do that. I'd rather we just returned it and left the area."

"We might not be able to," the leader said. "I've been following their videocasts and though I barely understand their language, there does seem to be concern about all the missing children. I've seen drawings which look very much like our shuttle, too. Somebody must have gotten careless on a few occasions and let themselves be seen. Any mistake bringing it back might be fatal."

"I wish we knew more about their expressions," the assistant sighed, "that way we might be better able to figure out if they were scared, angry, or, as you say, concerned. It's frustrating, sometimes, not to be able to tell."

"It is," he agreed. "Perhaps we'll be able to learn more from this one." The monitors showed that the subject had begun to play with the spaceship game again. "We should do more to learn their language. That way, at least, they might be more comfortable with us. I can't even tell if they're scared of us or not. Their expressions are so difficult to read."

"Don't get frustrated," his assistant cautioned. "Why don't you get some rest. I'll watch for a while before he goes to sleep."

"Are you sure?" he asked.

"It will be fine. I can handle it, really. There won't be any problems, I'm sure."

The leader rose to his feet. "Thanks. I appreciate it."

"You're welcome. Now, go." She pointed to the door. The leader bowed and left the room.

The room was full of toys.

It was almost as if they beckoned to him, even as he tried to sleep, tossing and turning on the bed they had supplied him with, a bed so very different from the one he was used to back home. The sleeping room was bare, containing nothing but the bed. It was the next room, the toy room, which had all of the fascinating things in it, all the toys and games, all of the colors, lights, and sounds. He had never played with them at night before, only during the day when the false sun that shone through the window lit up the room. He wondered if they watched him at night, if they'd notice if he sneaked into the other room and spent some time playing. Maybe he wasn't supposed to. Maybe the one he had spoken to earlier would come in and take the toys away or even hit him. He didn't think that it would ever hit him, but he wasn't sure.

He took a deep breath and stared at the ceiling. Surely it couldn't hurt if he spent a little bit of time with the spaceship game before getting back to sleep. Trying hard not to make a sound, he arose from the bed and walked slowly to the door. Opening it just enough to look through, he checked to be sure that there was nobody standing guard outside his door, nobody who would prevent him from entering the room. When he saw that he was alone, he realized that he had been holding his breath. He let it out with a long sigh and slipped into the room.

The toy room was quiet and dark. A few of the toys had small lights on them which helped to illumine the space a little bit. Other than that, there was no light at all, not even from the window. That was more proof that he must be in space. He was disappointed that it wasn't a real window, one he could look through and see his home spinning below. But if it wasn't a window, then it must be some kind of video screen. He wondered if there was something behind it, maybe some way to escape.

He spun around, searching for one of the wooden cubes. Getting down on his knees he shuffled across the floor, hands reaching out blindly in front of him, trying to imagine what would happen if he were able to break through the false window.

His hand closed around a cube. He stood and raised it, ready to throw as hard as he could. He hoped that none of them would hear the noise and come rushing through the door.

The door! He lowered his arm. Had the creature who'd talked to him before remembered to lock it when it left? Certainly opening the door would be much quieter than trying to get out by breaking the false window.

Keeping a firm grip on the cube, he slowly moved toward the door, trying not to kick any of the toys. He only remembered vaguely where it was and was surprised when, all of a sudden, he bumped face first into the wall. Gasping in surprise, he nearly dropped the cube before putting one hand against the wall and feeling for the door frame.

He hoped they couldn't hear his heart beating. He was sure that anybody listening would notice it. He forced himself to breathe slowly, and that helped to calm his nerves a little. He moved ever so slowly, wondering how long it would take to find the door.

Just as he was about to decide that he had begun to move the wrong way, he felt the cold metal of the frame. He'd found it! Wishing with all his might, he found the doorknob and turned it. The cold metal knob turned smoothly, meeting no resistance. He gasped. Slowly and quietly, he pushed, knowing that the fact that the knob turned didn't really mean that he wasn't locked in.

The door opened.

He poked his head out, not knowing what he would see. A long hallway stretched into the distance to his right and his left. Other doors appeared at regular intervals, but he had no idea what lay behind them. He wondered if there were others like him, others who had been taken against their will, others who had sleep rooms and toy rooms. For a moment he thought that he would try a few doors to see if they, too, were unlocked.

Then he realized that the doors could just as easily lead to other types of rooms, rooms in which his captors slept or worked. He didn't want to come across any of them, for he knew it would only mean his return to captivity. No, if he were going to help anybody else, if there *were* others to help, he had to find a way home.

He headed off to the right, hoping that it was the correct choice. The corridor was softly lit, although he couldn't tell where the light was coming from. After a few minutes, passing door after door, he came to an intersection. Making another guess, he turned right again and continued on his way. He didn't know what he was looking for. He only knew that when he found it, he'd know it.

It was not easy to remember all the turns he made, but he forced himself to do so, in case he had to retrace his steps to any previous point of his journey. He continued his wanderings, always peeking around corners to be sure he wasn't about to stumble into the arms of his captors. He passed doors too numerous to count, never stopping to see what was inside. Finally, he reached a point at which the corridor only went left or right, not allowing him to continue on as others had done.

He took the left-hand turn, picking up his pace a bit, more afraid by the moment that his absence would be discovered. As if in answer to his fears, red lights began to blink and a loud horn began to sound. He ran, hoping to find some place to hide before others came and discovered him in the halls. He noticed that the hall curved slightly, and he realized that he had reached the outer rim of the spaceship. He thought about heading back toward the center of the ship but, just as he decided to turn left again at the next intersection, he heard footsteps coming from that very corridor.

Suddenly, he saw an open door, located just ahead of the intersection. He ducked in and pressed himself up against the wall, shutting his eyes, waiting for the footsteps to fade into the distance. Only when all he could hear was the blood pounding in his ears did he dare open his eyes.

What he saw pleased and surprised him beyond his wildest dreams. There, before him, was a small shuttle of some sort, its hatch open. He clambered aboard, thinking that it would be a good place to hide. Yet he couldn't help but look at the controls, sitting in the pilot's chair. He was amazed that he was able to recognize the basic controls. They were identical to the controls on the game he'd been playing in the toy room!

He pushed a few buttons and was rewarded with the sound of the craft's engines starting up. Another button and the door closed. A gentle moving of the joystick and the shuttle lifted up off the ground. Now all that he had to do was fly it home. He hoped that it would react the way the ship in the game did.

The space doors were closed, though, and he knew that they wouldn't simply open for him. It was time to resort to force. Although the game's controls were simpler, the important functions seemed to be in the same place on this ship. Remembering the button on the game which fired the laser cannon, he pressed down hard on it and the weapon fired at the door, blasting a hole large enough for the shuttle to fly through. The sudden pressure change, however, sucked the ship toward the jagged gash in the hull of the ship. It was all he could do to keep the little shuttle from scraping on one of the metal edges as the ship soared out through the opening.

Once he had cleared the hole, the ride became much smoother and he pushed the joystick forward in order to pick up speed. He wasn't sure if the big ship would fire on him or not, but he didn't want to take any chances, either. Putting as much distance between the ship and the shuttle was definitely the first goal.

Pushing another button brought up a view of the receding spaceship on his monitor. He was pleased to see that no other ships had been launched to intercept him, and more pleased that no laser cannons were evident which could blast his ship apart before he managed to pilot it into the atmosphere. If, that was, he could navigate it properly and not burn up as it entered.

Switching back to a forward view, he saw the telltale haze which showed the top of the atmosphere. He had seen enough pictures taken from satellites to recognize it for what it was. He wondered if the ship was going too fast or too slow to make the entrance safely, and knew that there was only one way for him to find out.

Just as he was about to move the stick for a reentry, the ship made a course correction on its own. He felt the little craft speed up a bit and dip a few degrees. At the same time he heard a voice.

"Hello," it said. He recognized it as belonging to the alien who had come to visit him earlier, the one he had told that he wanted to go home. "If you are hearing this, then my plans for you have worked. I know you might not understand this, but I'm glad you're going home. You're not like the others I've seen. You're smarter, faster to figure things out. I didn't want anything to happen to you, and I didn't want to be a part of anything which would bring you harm."

He felt the heat in the cabin rising as the shuttle rode through the atmosphere, amazed that anybody would have taken the time to help him escape. The ship unerringly glided through the lower atmosphere. He could see clouds below, and the outline of his country. The ship maneuvered itself, dropping swiftly out of the sky. It seemed to be aiming for the sparsely populated center of his country, the place he lived, far from the large cities of the coast.

"Soon you will be home," the voice continued, "and you'll be free to live your own life. I think that you have a wonderful future in front of you. As for me, when they find out what I did for you, they'll send me back to my own home. I hope that you won't forget me."

"I won't," he said, though he knew that it couldn't hear him. The ship was much closer to the ground now. He could see the outlines of roads and streams.

"This ship will land in an empty field near your house. You must leave the ship as fast as you can. Although I am probably wrong to help you, I still do not think that it is time for your people to know how it works. There is, however, one small piece of our technology which I am happy to give to you."

He did not know how people wouldn't learn about the ship, and he did not know what "technology" meant. Before he could think too much about it, though, a panel opened in the console. There, nestled within, was the spaceship game with which he had entertained himself. He reached in and removed it, flicking it on to be sure that he wasn't imagining things. A light glowed, indicating that it was operating properly.

"I'm sure that if you tell people what happened to you, they won't listen, won't believe that you were captured by an alien race and kept on our ship. In case anybody *does* believe you, though, tell them that we come from a place we call 'Earth' and that we call ourselves 'humans.' We've been watching your people, your planet, for a number of years, and we'll be making contact with your leaders soon. Before that, though, we needed to know more about you."

When he next looked up, his ship was approaching the field, coming in with the sun behind it in order to help mask its existence. A moment later, it landed with a thump. The hatch opened and he grabbed the game, moving away from the shuttle as quickly as he could.

"I have to go now," the voice said, although there was nobody left in the ship to hear. "I'll never forget you. I hope that you can forgive us."

He raced to the edge of the field, arriving just in time to turn around and see the shuttle explode in a blaze of yellow and crimson flames. He held on tight to the game, knowing that it was the only thing that might help him prove what had happened to him, prove that there were others in the universe, prove that he wasn't making up stories. He had his game.

And that was all he needed.

NIGHT OF THE BALL

by Greg LaBarbera

I stood in the meadow, huddling in my overcoat. Silvery moonlight crept across the ground, casting eerie shadows on tall grasses. Tufts of steam blew from my mouth like smoke. Autumn had definitely come early to the small town of Oakley. I pulled my handheld tape recorder from my pocket and clicked RECORD.

"It's one of those nights," I said. "A night when something is in the air. A night when anything can happen."

My sister, Jena, rolled her eyes. "I know what you're doing, James. Aren't you a little old to be playing detective?"

Exasperated, I clicked the OFF button. "Now I have to start over. I don't want your goofy voice on my tape." I waved the recorder in front of her nose. "And the name isn't James. It's Jimmy-the-Taper."

With a look on her face as if she were touching stinky socks, Jena eased my hand away. "Why do you call yourself Jimmy-the-Taper?" She smirked. "Is it because you have a pointed head?"

I could feel blood pounding in my ears. Ever since Jena started junior high, she thought she was cooler than a penguin. "You know why. It's because I use this tape recorder to help solve all my cases."

"Ha!" she laughed. "What cases? You haven't solved anything tougher than a two-plus-two math problem."

I took off my baseball cap so I could get nose to nose

with her. "Oh yeah?" I said. "What about the case of the ghost in Stephanie Watkins' house?"

She pushed me back a little. "That wasn't a ghost, you goofball. That was her cat having kittens in the basement."

"At least I solved the case." I grabbed a small card from my pocket and handed it to Jena. "Ever since then I've been officially open for business."

She read the words I'd scribbled in black Magic Marker. "Jimmy-the-Taper Detective Agency: Specializing in the Paranormal." She rolled her eyes again and handed me the card. "You're only in fourth grade. You don't even know what 'paranormal' means."

"I do, too. It means things like ghosts and UFOs and aliens. Stuff that isn't normal." I grinned. "Maybe I should be investigating *you*."

Before I could stop her, Jena snatched the tape recorder out of my hand. "Well, let me give you a bit of information on my case." She clicked RECORD and said, "You're an idiot." Then she dropped the recorder in my pocket and spun around, swinging her long red hair into my face.

As I stood there, spitting out a few strands of Jena's hair, she turned and said, "I think Dad is finished setting up your telescope. And by the way, take off his bathrobe. I've told you a dozen times it doesn't look like a detective's trenchcoat."

As much as I hated to admit it, Jena was right. I looked more like a redheaded, four-foot-tall bear than a detective.

I clicked REWIND. The tape whirled backward, sounding like a bunch of frantic chipmunks. Bleep-diddle-bleep-diddle-bleep. I pushed PLAY and heard Jena's voice:

You're an idiot. Bleep-diddle-bleep-diddle-bleep. *You're an idiot.*

Looking down at the bathrobe, I shook my head. "I've *got* to get a real overcoat."

I ran to the car and quickly changed into my jean jacket. I could hardly wait to try out my new telescope as I jogged back toward the meadow. My dad was already peering through the lens.

"Too bad your mother is giving that presentation at the university this weekend," he said. "This is a perfect night for stargazing."

"This can't be much fun for you, Dad," I said. "You work with the biggest telescopes in the state."

He looked over his shoulder, toward an observatory that sat on the highest hill in Oakley. A few satellite dishes flanked the building, looking like giant lasers ready to fend off alien attackers.

"This is definitely more fun," he said. "Do you know how hard it is to carry that thing around?" He winked and I smiled.

I looked through the telescope again and gasped.

"What is it now?" asked Jena. "Is the moon really a giant cheese ball?"

A chill raced up my legs and into the middle of my back as I watched a bluish-silver light race toward us. "I don't know about that," I yelled, "but something is heading this way!"

In two seconds, a humongous UFO hovered over us.

With his hand on our shoulders, my father silently drew us toward the edge of the meadow. "Take it easy, kids."

Jena's eyes were bigger than the time she saw the designer sweaters on sale at the mall.

The UFO just floated there, in midair.

"It looks like a shiny, blue, baseball stadium," I said.

An opening appeared in the side. A long ramp slid down to the ground. As if on cue, a giant silver ball, as big as a house, teetered on top of the ramp. Without taking my eyes from the UFO, I whispered, "Do you think they want a game with the high school team?"

"This is no time to be funny," Jena hissed.

Finally, I got my wits back and grabbed my tape recorder. A deep moaning came from the UFO. I clicked RECORD and got the tail end of the sound on my tape.

Suddenly, the ball raced down the ramp. As soon as it hit the ground, the UFO disappeared in a flash of wind and heat.

We watched as the big ball just sat there. I clicked STOP.

"What do you think it is?" Jena whispered, her voice quavering. "What's it doing here?"

My father just shook his head.

My hand trembled, but I think it was from awe and excitement as much as fear. "I don't know," I said, "but I intend to find out. This is the case I've been waiting for. The Case of the Big Silver Ball from Outer Space."

Without warning, the ball began rolling erratically around the meadow as if searching for something, leaving giant troughs in the ground. Every now and then the ball would make a long, deep, droning similar to the sound that came from the UFO. I held the recorder out to catch it on tape.

"I don't know if I like the looks of this," said my father. The ball began picking up speed.

And then it turned straight toward us.

"Run!" Dad yelled.

We sprinted toward the car, dove in, and peeled out. I gasped as the ball ran over the spot where we'd just been parked, then moved on. With an earsplitting crack, it splintered a pine tree.

We sped back into town, up the hill that led to the observatory, and came to a skidding stop in the parking lot. My father eyed a black moped parked next to the door.

"Good," he said. "Devin's here."

We ran through the doorway, down the corridor, and burst into the main lab. All kinds of screens flashed and beeped. Overhead, the roof was retracted, leaving a hole for the giant telescope. The sky looked clear. Devin McKenzie, my dad's research partner, was hammering away at the push-button phone. Letting loose an exasperated breath, she slammed down the receiver.

"Did you see that UFO, Devin?" I asked.

She didn't answer me, but turned to my father. "I saw it, all right, but not until it was right on top of us. None of our equipment picked it up. When I tried to call the offices at the Capitol I found out all communications are down."

"It might be the low frequency coming from that ball," Dad said.

Devin rubbed her forehead. "Could be. Who knows?"

"Where is it now?" Not waiting for an answer, my father ran through a doorway and out onto the balcony. Devin, Jena, and I followed close behind.

From atop the hill we could see the meadow and town below. The big ball had laid a path of broken trees that wound around the woods. Presently, it was crashing into some houses on the edge of Oakley, leaving their walls in crunched heaps of rubble. Somehow news of the danger had already spread. The streets were filled with cars speeding out of town.

"What is it, Dad?" asked Jena.

"Maybe we're under attack," I said. "There could be balls like this all over the world."

"Attack?" said Jena. "Why would they choose Oakley?"

"They probably heard about you and figured this would be a good place to start."

Jena glared at me.

Dad said, "Let's not jump to conclusions. One thing's for sure, though: We're not going to get help unless we figure out how to get communications back."

Devin nodded and ran back into the observatory, my father at her heels.

As soon as they were gone, I said, "Let's go, Jena."

"Where?"

"Back to town. I can't solve the case of the big ball from here. I have an idea on how to stop it, and I don't know how to drive a moped. So let's go."

She stared at me like I'd grown a second head. "No way, James. I'm staying right here. You heard Dad."

I knew what she was thinking, but I'd show her—I'd solve the case and be a hero. So I crossed my arms and shot her my coolest detective look, the one where I squint a little bit with one eye.

"Well," I said, "I guess I'll have to tell him you almost drained your savings account to buy those cool Hammerton jeans everybody is wearing."

She stepped close to me with clenched fists. "You wouldn't dare."

"I would. And I will." I knew I had her. Not only would she drive me, but she'd be forced to witness my success. I smiled wickedly.

Jena shook her head and mumbled, "I can't believe I'm going to do this."

"Let's go, then. If the ball doesn't decide to go backward it should eventually reach Park Road."

With Jena trailing behind me, we crept out into the parking lot, cranked up Devin's moped, and sped toward town. Making a face like I'd just swallowed a bug, I wrapped my arms around Jena's waist.

We rode through the deserted streets, past broken houses and smashed cars, all the handiwork of the big ball from outer space. Over the wind, I shouted, "Take us to the school!"

While Jena drove, I pulled out my recorder. I rewound the tape a bit. Bleep-diddle-bleep-diddle-bleep. I clicked RECORD. "The big ball seems to move in a random fashion with unpredictable stops and starts. Also, a low frequency comes from the ball every so often. The sound is recorded earlier on the tape."

In a few moments, we were parked next to the back door leading into Mrs. Daniel's classroom. I took out my mini screwdriver set. I looked around.

"The coast is clear," I whispered. Then I added, "I never thought I'd try to break *into* the school."

Jena stood there, her arms crossed. Leaves scraped cartwheels across the playground. "What are you doing?" she asked.

"I'm going to pick the lock."

Jena picked up a rock. "We don't have time for this."

I flinched when the sound of shattering glass filled the night. Then I peered over my shoulder. "The coast is still clear."

Reaching through the hole in the window, Jena unlocked the door from inside. "There you go, Inspector Gadget."

I stood staring at her. "I hope we don't have to pay for that."

"Just get going!" she yelled.

We ran inside. I started rifling through the cabinets.

"What are you looking for?" Jena asked.

"This," I said, as I pulled a box out of a tall cabinet. "Six gallons of superstrength glue. Remember when I got some on my hand and my hand got stuck in Carmen Montoya's hair? Mrs. Daniel had to cut Carmen's hair and I had to soak my hand in acetone for over an hour."

Jena folded her arms. "You're going to stop that ball with glue."

"Yeah. We'll pour this all over the road, and when the big ball rolls by it'll get stuck."

Jena slowly nodded her head. "Now I'm sure of it. You *are* nuts."

"You're just jealous because you didn't think of it first."

A squealing sound came from the corner of the room and

I spun around, my heart doing a tap dance on my chest.

It was only Henry, our class guinea pig. The turtles, Bow and Arrow, and Mel-the-Mouse gazed at us from their cages.

"I guess we woke them up," I said. "Do you think we should take them with us?"

Jena shook her head. "The way that ball is rolling all over town they're probably just as safe here. Anyway, I'm not going to carry a couple of slimy turtles."

I nodded and we hopped back on the moped and sped across town. As I'd suspected, the ball hadn't reached Park Road yet. All the houses were still standing. In the distance I heard the droning of the ball, the crack of splintering wood, and the scream of twisting metal.

"Here's a good spot," I said. "Hurry!"

Jena and I each took three gallon jugs of glue and sloshed them across the street in one glistening puddle. When we finished I tossed the containers to the side of the road and wrung my hands together. "That's enough glue to stop an elephant."

Jena pointed down the street. "Here it comes!"

"Take cover!" I shouted, and we squatted behind the biggest oak tree on the block.

Light from streetlamps flashed off the ball's silver surface as it made its way down Park Road. It rolled almost straight down the street, stopping once to crush a minivan. As it got closer to the glue pool Jena took a step from behind the tree.

"Do you see that?" she said. "Look at the cats."

About ten of the neighborhood cats seemed to appear

at once, hissing and spitting as the ball rolled by. One even started chasing it!

"Maybe they think it's a giant yarn ball," I said.

Turning from the cats, I held my breath as the ball rolled into the glue. It stopped right in the middle of the puddle. I jumped up in the air and started doing my best victory dance. "Got it! Chalk up another case for Jimmy-the-Taper!"

Jena tapped me on the shoulder and I froze in mid-jig. She thrust her chin out toward the street and said, "Not so fast, Sherlock."

The ball began rumbling down Park Road again. But now it had superstrength glue smeared all over one side. As it zigzagged along the street the ball began picking up leaves and scraps of paper. Soon it looked like a rolling trash pile.

With my jaw hanging and my arms still in the air, I said, "It didn't work."

"Not only that," Jena shouted, "but it caught one of Mrs. Jefferson's cats!"

Sure enough, a kitten was stuck to the side of the ball, screeching and flailing, spinning 'round and 'round as the ball headed down the street.

"Oh no," I groaned. "Cat pancake."

We hopped back on the moped and gave chase. We followed the sphere for two blocks.

Jena yelled, "We've got to stop it!"

And then just like that the ball came to rest on the Jenkin's front lawn, the kitten dangling about six feet off the ground.

We parked the moped at the side of the street and I said, "Go get it off."

Jena whispered through clenched teeth, as if any noise would start the big ball rolling again. "That glue was *your* idea. *You* get it off."

"I would, but you're taller. I won't be able to reach."

After giving me a look that would burn holes through metal, Jena turned around and inched toward the ball. The kitten just hung there and whimpered. Wind gusted. A piece of newspaper stuck to the side of the ball and flapped. Jena reached up, and the ball groaned as it teetered toward her, then back. I gasped.

Jena choked down a terrified squeal. She looked like a bug next to a grapefruit. I clenched my hands into tight, shaking fists. As much as my sister was annoying me lately, I didn't want to see her crushed into a pile of goo. Time seemed to stand still on the deserted road. Then, in one swift motion, Jena snatched the kitten and dashed across the street. I let loose my breath and the ball started rolling away. Soon it was gone.

Bent over, resting one hand on her knee, Jena caught her breath. Then she stopped and examined the kitten in her hand.

"That was close," I said. "The glue mustn't have dried yet." Jena just stood there, tapping her foot, staring at me.

"What?" I said.

She thrust her arm out, hand extended. The kitten hung there stuck to her palm. "That's what," she said.

Even if my lips were super-glued together I couldn't have stopped myself from laughing. I sat down on the curb, clutching my stomach. Jena gently shook her hand, a look on her face like she had nose slime on her fingers. I laughed even harder.

"This is your fault, James," she growled. "That was the dumbest idea you've ever had. You stink as a detective."

"I don't see *you* coming up with anything."

She sat down next to me, one hand under her chin, the other in her lap. Now that the kitten was safe from the big ball, it didn't seem to mind being stuck to Jena's hand. It purred while it rested on her thigh.

"Well, if *I* were a detective," Jena said, "I'd at least listen to the stuff on my tape. Maybe I'd get some ideas from it."

I hated when Jena was right.

"That's just what I was thinking," I said as I dug the recorder out of my pocket. I pushed the PLAY button.

Bleep-diddle-bleep-diddle-bleep. . . . *random fashion with unpredictable stops and starts. Also, a low frequency comes from the ball every so often. The sound is recorded—*

I stopped the tape and bolted upright. "That's it! The frequency! I think I have a way to stop it."

"I hope so," said Jena. "Dad has surely noticed we're gone by now." She looked into her lap. "And how am I going to get this . . . this kitten off my hand?"

"Don't worry about that now. Come on. We've got to get to the house."

We sped through the deserted streets of town, the kitten dangling over the moped's handlebar as Jena tried to steer. When we reached our house I crashed through the front door, bounded up the stairs, snatched a box from my closet, then raced back down to the driveway. Jena was waiting on the moped, cradling the kitten in her jacket. I shoved the box toward her. "What is it?"

I shot her a cool smile and nodded. "It's the universal remote for my remote control cars."

"Are you crazy? You're going to try to steer the big ball? The same ball that's making a junk heap out of Oakley?"

"Yep. See here?" I pointed to the print scrolled across the bottom of the box. "Works on all frequencies."

Jena tried to rub her chin and got a mouthful of cat fur. "Ugh. Let's just get going. It seems like a better idea than pouring glue all over the street."

We searched Oakley. All over were signs of the big ball's path of destruction—crumpled trees, big troughs through yards and parks, crushed cars, and sparking wires dangling from angled telephone poles. Near the edge of town I saw a line of treetops shuddering.

"It's heading back toward the observatory," I said.

In a few minutes we stood in the middle of a darkened street. Jena had parked the moped in the woods. Slowly, I extended the antenna on the remote control and clicked on the power. Soon, the sphere came rumbling down the road, moonlight glinting off its side. Since its trip around town, the ball had gathered more things on its sticky surface: some aluminum cans, part of a mailbox, even an old tire.

"Here it comes," said Jena.

The kitten puffed up its fur and hissed.

I pointed the remote at the ball and turned the mini steering wheel. Nothing happened.

Jena's voice quivered. "I-it's not w-working."

"It has to be closer," I lied. Hopefully Jena didn't hear the uncertainty in my voice. Since the glue incident I desperately wanted this to work. I had to prove to her I could solve the case.

My hands began to sweat as the ball closed in on us. I shook the control. "Come on. Come on."

Then it happened. I spun the wheel to the right. The ball moved right. I spun the wheel to the left. The ball turned left. My heart flew up into my throat.

"It's working!" I said. "It's working!"

Jena yelled, "You're doing it, James!"

The kitten kept hissing.

I pushed the little stick back, the one that makes the cars go in reverse.

The ball kept coming.

We started edging backward as I frantically pushed the lever.

"It's *not* working!" Jena cried. "It's *not* working!"

Soon we were running as the ball picked up speed and thundered straight toward us. Every time we turned it turned with us.

Jena screamed, "You idiot! You probably made it mad or something!"

I glanced over my shoulder and gasped. The ball thudded about ten feet from our heels. I dropped the remote. The ball smashed it into a million little pieces. Now my lungs were screaming, my legs wobbly.

I huffed and pointed straight ahead. "The . . . fire . . . house."

We dashed into the open truck bay. A giant crash followed us as the ball hit the front of the building. A few bricks crumbled and smacked the concrete floor. The ball sat outside, looking like the silver eye of a giant alien.

Jena shivered next to me. "Do you think it's going to wait for us?"

I shrugged and leaned forward. "Nobody's home!" I called.

The ball pounded against the fire house again.

"Way to go," Jena shouted.

We huddled together as the building groaned. A shower of bricks and smoke filled the truck bay. When the dust finally settled, we were met by silence. We had our arms wrapped around each other. Jena's eyes were wide with fear. Her whole body shook as she held on to me. For once I didn't feel like cringing.

"Are you all right?" I asked.

Tight-lipped, Jena answered, "Yeah, I'm okay."

"Let's get the moped, then. Third time is the charm. Are you with me?"

Jena shook her head. "No, James. I'm going back to the observatory."

The kitten sneezed a little puff of dust.

I looked at the fur ball stuck to her hand and snickered. "Come on, Jena. What are you—a fraidy-cat?"

"You think everything is a big joke, don't you?" Jena shot back. "I can't believe I let you talk me into this. First, I help you take Devin's moped." She thrust her hand out. It was trembling with anger. "Then, you get this cat stuck to me." Then she screamed, "And *then*, you almost get me crushed by a giant pinball!" Tears glistened in the corners of her eyes. "You're the worst detective on the planet."

Silently she hurried out of the fire house and made her way toward the road leading up the hill. I stood there among the bricks and dust, going through the night's events in my mind.

Jena was right. Who was I kidding? I really wasn't a detective. Everything had been a total disaster. We were both lucky to be in one piece.

With slumped shoulders, I reached into my pocket and took out my tape recorder. I hit REWIND.

Bleep-diddle-bleep-diddle-bleep. *You're an idiot.*

By the time I caught up to her, Jena was already halfway up the hill.

"I'm sorry," I said.

She didn't even look at me. "Whatever."

The rest of the way up the hill I kept my mouth shut, quietly trailing behind her. I think it was the longest time my sister and I hadn't said a word to each other. I kept softly playing her voice over and over on my tape.

Bleep-diddle-bleep-diddle-bleep. *You're an idiot.* Bleep-diddle-bleep-diddle-bleep. *You're an idiot.*

Then my thumb slipped, and I accidentally hit FAST FORWARD instead of REWIND.

Bleep-diddle-bleep-diddle-bleep-*later, Fizgig . . . squeak-squeak-squeak.*

I froze. "Did you hear that? A voice said 'later, Fizgig.' Then there was that squeaking sound." I rewound the tape and hit FAST FORWARD again. Bleep-diddle-bleep-diddle-bleep-*later, Fizgig . . . squeak-squeak-squeak.*

"Yeah. So what?" said Jena. "You probably had your tape recorder on when we were in Mrs. Daniel's classroom. That's just Henry and Mel squeaking in their cages."

I grabbed her jacket. "When you hear the words and the squeaking the tape is running fast-forward." I rewound the tape and punched PLAY. "Listen now." The deep moaning of the UFO came out of the speaker, followed by the droning of the ball.

Again, Jena said, "So what? On fast-forward the big ball sounds just like your class pets."

"That doesn't explain the words 'later, Fizgig.' "

"It's a coincidence, Agent Numskull."

"Is *this* a coincidence?" I pushed RECORD and made some long, deep, moaning sounds. Then I rewound the tape. Instead of hitting PLAY I clicked FAST FORWARD. The words came out muddled but you could understand them.

Jena is a big doofus.

"Very funny." With one hand on her hip, she pointed her finger at me. I was staring straight at the kitten's nose. "You'll never learn, Joke Boy."

"Don't you get it, Jena?" I said. "I might know how to communicate with them. They just speak real slow. That's why we were able to understand those words when the tape ran fast-forward."

Jena spoke to me at a turtle's pace. "Why . . . don't . . . you . . . tell . . . them . . . to . . . come . . . down . . . and . . . pick . . . you . . . up . . . and . . . take . . . you . . . away?" Then she turned and marched up the hill.

I didn't follow. Instead, I stared into space, trying to put everything together. Jena had been right. All night I'd been playing detective. Now I was starting to *think* like one.

I said to myself, "A zigzagging ball. Freaked-out cats. Words and squeaking on the tape when it runs fast-forward." My jaw dropped low enough to fit an orange in my mouth. "It couldn't be," I said. "No way." Then I shouted, "I've got it, Jena! I think I've got it!"

She groaned. "What is it *this* time?"

I ran past her and called over my shoulder, "You wouldn't believe me if I told you. Just come on."

Panting, I crashed through the door of the observatory.

Devin yelled, "Thank goodness!"

My father said, "Where have you been?"

"Dad, show me how to send a voice message into space. I think I know how to stop the big ball."

Putting his hand on my shoulder he said, "James, we don't have time for you to play detective."

I shook his hand off. "Dad, I'm serious. Really."

Maybe it was the tone of my voice, but my dad hustled me to a microphone that was surrounded by screens and flashing buttons. He pushed a button, flicked a switch, then nodded. "Go ahead."

I put the tape recorder up to the microphone and played the deep, droning sound that came from the ball. Then I made a series of long, drawn-out sounds of my own. When I finished, I flicked the switch. "That's it."

My father stared at me, his brow furrowed. Devin had a look on her face like she was ready to call the loony bin to come get me.

I shrugged my shoulders. "What?"

A few moments later, Jena came charging into the room. "They're back! Another ship is coming!"

We all ran out to the balcony. Sure enough, another UFO, twice the size of the one that came earlier, hovered over the meadow. We stood frozen, our breaths held. The sound of scraping metal shrieked through the night as a giant doorway appeared in the side of the silver-blue UFO.

Jena whispered, "What have you done, James? They could roll hundreds of balls from that opening."

Silently, I crossed my fingers. My heart beat up into my throat. Could I have been wrong? Could I have brought even more destruction to the Earth?

Two giant aliens appeared. One alien was tugging a shorter one by the ear.

Everyone stepped back, our heads tilted up. They stood taller than the observatory on top of the hill. Two almond-shaped eyes gazed from the middle of their noseless faces. They almost looked human, except for the two wriggling digits at the end of their hands and their long tendril-like silver hair. The bigger alien pointed at the ball. The smaller reached down and picked it up.

"What are they doing?" whispered Jena.

No one answered as the smaller alien removed the top of the sphere.

Everyone's jaws—except mine, of course—made a trip to the floor. Me, I just sighed with relief. A monstrous, fuzzy animal poked out from the top of the ball. It looked like a two-headed hamster with four black eyes sticking up from each head. Both noses sniffed the air, twitching.

Head hung low, the smaller alien shuffled back into the ship. The taller looked at us apologetically and shrugged. Then, for over a minute, it made a bunch of groaning sounds. I made sure I got it all on tape. Finally, the alien ducked back into the ship. As before, the UFO disappeared in a cloud of wind and heat.

In the stillness that followed, everyone turned toward me, their faces contorted with confusion. My father said, "How did you—"

"Just good detective work, Dad." I smiled at my sister. "Jena gave me the idea. I just asked them to come pick up their pet."

I rewound the tape. Instead of hitting PLAY to hear the alien's slow, groaning language, I pushed FAST FORWARD so we could hear the message clearly.

Sorry about my son, Blork. Last month he left his pet Fizgig and that running ball on Saturn. You should have seen the damage to their Dangerian Mountain Range. He'll be grounded for the rest of the millennium for this.

Shaking his head, my father clapped me on the back. "I can't believe it, Jame—I mean Jimmy-the-Taper. You solved the case."

Nodding, I crossed my arms and grinned.

Then my father turned to my sister. "Jena? Why is there a kitten stuck to your hand?"

A week later, everyone was still cleaning up the damage, and I'd just gotten another case from Stephanie Watkins.

I walked into my room to get my tape recorder and

stopped short. A large box rested on my bed. Jena had hardly said a word to me since the case of the big ball. I had been looking over my shoulder the whole week, waiting for her revenge. This could be it.

I tapped the box with my finger. Nothing happened. So I tore off the top and dove for cover. After a moment, I peeked over the edge of the box.

"Whoa," I whispered. A gray trenchcoat was folded neatly among some tissue paper. A note was attached to the receipt: NOT BAD FOR A FOURTH GRADER. CONSIDER YOURSELF AN OFFICIAL DETECTIVE.

I was ready to race down stairs to thank my father. Then I glanced at the receipt. Scribbled in the middle were the words: EXCHANGE: ONE PAIR OF HAMMERTON JEANS FOR ONE TRENCHCOAT.

I pulled the overcoat on and raced toward Jena's room. She was lounging on her bed, reading. She eyed me over a copy of *Cool Teen* magazine.

"Thanks, Jena. I can't believe you did this!" I turned around in a slow circle. "You know, we *did* make a pretty good team. And I was thinking . . . how would you like to be my permanent assistant?"

Her pillow plastered me in the face before I saw it coming.

SPIRITS FROM THE VASTY DEEP

by John Morressy

Afancs were terrible things to work with. Huge and wet and hairy they were, always ill-tempered and noisy and rude. They took particular pleasure in materializing in a wizard's chamber the very instant a spell was done, waving a spear and shouting threats and getting water and weeds and muck all over things. That was your typical afanc notion of fun. Kedrigern hated summoning them up, or working with them. He did not even like to think about them.

But everything in this world has its place, and so do things in the worlds beyond. There was nothing like an afanc for dealing with fire demons. Those wretched things could have you ringed with flame as tight as a baby in a blanket, but turn an afanc loose on them, and before a generous pinch of sand had gone through the glass, there was nothing left but steam and a charred spot here and there. Afancs worked every time.

All the same, thought the wizard as he took his spelling book down from the shelf, it's far wiser not to get mixed up with fire demons in the first place. Anyone who does has no one to blame but himself.

His present client was a perfect example: just because one is known as Troam of the Terrible Temper, one can't call a sorceress nasty names and expect to get away with it. This experience probably wouldn't improve Troam's temper either, however it worked out. Sighing and shaking his head at the human condition, Kedrigern laid the speller on his worktable, opened the book with care, and set to his work.

The spell for summoning an afanc was complex and subtle, as one might expect of any magic dealing with a Celtic water-spirit. What with half the words being unpronounceable and the other half sounding just enough like something else to keep him confused and stumbling, it was a full, and difficult, day's work simply to get everything organized.

By midafternoon he had had enough of it and needed a break. He rang for his house-troll, ordered a mug of cold ale to be brought out to the comfortable chair under the oaks, and slipped from the house as quietly as possible so as not to disturb his wife. Princess had recently discovered the virtues of the afternoon nap, and as he sat under the trees, waiting for his ale, Kedrigern reflected that she was probably the only sensible member of the household.

Spot burst from the house on great flat feet and skidded to a halt at its master's side with a cry of "Yah, yah!" Despite its headlong speed, it had not spilled a drop of ale.

"Well done, Spot. Quick, but careful. That's the way."

"Yah?"

"Nothing else, thank you," said the wizard, taking the beaded tankard. "You may as well find yourself a cool place and rest until dinnertime."

"Yah!" said the little troll, bouncing up and down in glee. Its ears flapped audibly.

"No sense all of us drudging away in this heat," said Kedrigern, leaning back with a martyred sigh. "I'll carry on alone."

Spot left him, and he reclined for a time, eyes closed, idly half-listening to the stitch and tick of insects, the distant birdcalls, the faint rustle of the upper branches in the mild afternoon breeze. It was very restful, and far more pleasant than the stuffy confines of his workroom. He was sorely tempted to surrender to the day and drift into sleep, letting Troam sweat and sizzle for a few hours more.

But a promise was a promise; a commitment was a commitment. More to the point, a client was a client and a fee was a fee, and Troam's messenger had paid generously in advance. One could ask no greater proof of urgency.

Kedrigern hitched himself up a bit, took a sip of the cold ale, and faced his obligations. A quarter of an hour's rest, no more, and then back to work. When that fat white cloud reached the edge of the grove, he would rise and return to his labors.

He took a deeper draft, observed a bee making its rounds, studied with delight a hummingbird that hovered just beyond his reach, and then checked the progress of the white cloud. It seemed to have grown a bit, but moved no nearer to the grove of aspen.

Looking at it more closely, Kedrigern saw that it was a very smooth and unusually shiny cloud. Instead of drifting lazily eastward, as all the other clouds were doing, it was coming toward him. This was decidedly uncloudlike behavior.

He reached in his tunic and drew out the silver medallion of his guild. Raising it to his eye, he peered through the Aperture of True Vision and gave a little gasp of surprise. The cloud was not a cloud. It was a bowl-shaped thing of white metal, and it appeared to be making for a landing in the meadow before the house.

This had to be the work of an afanc. Who but a Celtic water-spirit would travel in something shaped like a big bowl? And only an afanc would have the effrontery to anticipate a spell and arrive ahead of time and in its own vehicle. Kedrigern gulped the remaining ale and climbed resolutely to his feet, jaw set firmly, brow furrowed in wrath. This afanc would learn that Kedrigern of Silent Thunder Mountain was not a wizard to be trifled with.

The flying bowl descended smoothly and silently. It was much larger than it had first appeared—the size of a small castle, at least. The afanc must have brought its tarn along with it, Kedrigern thought, his anger growing. That great bowl would leave an awful dent in his meadow. The nerve of the creature was galling.

About twenty feet from the ground, the bowl slowed. At ten feet it stopped and hovered noiselessly. There was a click and a soft whirr, and five absurdly spindly legs slid from the bottom of the thing to plant broad, rounded bases on the ground. White spots around the bowl began to glow brightly, several of them flickering in vivid colors. The air around Kedrigern grew tingly, as if charged with powerful enchantment.

This seemed to smack of more than mere afancs. It might well be that Adajeva, the sorceress who had beset Troam with fire demons, had learned of Kedrigern's work and was trying to undermine it. And she might be assisted by others. Like any wizard, Kedrigern had made enemies, sometimes without knowing. Whatever the case, there was no point in being foolhardy. He worked a quick but powerful short-term, all-purpose protective spell and stood with arms folded and expression dour, awaiting the appearance of the afanc.

The side of the bowl opened, and a long, broad ramp unfolded itself like a black tongue and came to the ground a few paces before him. Kedrigern did not move or alter his expression. After a silent moment, two figures began to descend the ramp. They did not walk, as men would, nor did they flow on watery steeds, as would afancs. Indeed, they did nothing at all. The ramp itself moved, bringing them to the ground a few paces from the wizard.

They were very ugly, even for afancs. They had bowls over their heads filled with a murky soup through which their faces appeared to be a putrid purplish blue-green, with patches of yellowy gray. They had wide, slobbery mouths and far too many eyes. And arms. And fingers. They were not hairy in the typical afanc way—not visibly, at least, since they were covered head to foot in what looked like cloth of gold. A rather sumptuous outfit, the wizard thought, for a water-spirit. They had no feet at all, and no discernible legs, only a kind of columnar trunk rounded off at the bottom. They floated in the air, unmoving, about a forearm's length above the ramp, looking at the wizard. Showing off their shoddy magic, he thought, and sniffed.

"I suppose you think this is very clever. Very witty. Ever so droll," Kedrigern said coldly.

Several of the outermost arms of the left-hand afanc twitched slightly. The other afanc started to drift to one side, but brought itself back into place at once. Neither of them spoke or attempted to communicate with the wizard.

"Well, I'm not amused. Do you hear that, you two? Kedrigern is not the least bit amused," he went on. "You can tell that to Adajeva, too, and whoever else put you up to this. And you can tell them I won't forget."

The afancs slowly turned to face each other. Inside their helmets, their features moved and light flickered. They appeared to be communicating with one another and ignoring Kedrigern. Angered by this new rudeness, he became caustic.

"Look at yourselves. Ridiculous. Do you hear me? You look ridiculous. Cloth of gold, like a pair of mincing court fops. And those silly glass bowls over your heads don't help either. What's the matter—ashamed of being all wet and hairy and drippy? Well, I can't blame you for that, but you might have dressed yourselves in something more becoming—like a greasy old washrag. And where are your horses, and your spears? What kind of afancs—"

"You speak our language," a flat, tinny voice said.

"Don't interrupt me when I'm ranting!" Kedrigern cried. "Of course I speak your language. How else can I tell you what I think of this ludicrous performance of yours—flying about in an oversized washtub, dressed up like a pair of clowns with arms and fingers all over the place and no feet—"

"How do you speak our language? You wear no translating machine," the voice broke in.

"I don't need a translating machine, whatever that is. I don't need any machine to speak your language or anyone else's," said Kedrigern. "Machines are nothing but big, clumsy things that creak and rattle and break down when you need them most and end up a heap of firewood. Machines are as stupid and unreliable as afancs, which brings me back—"

"Where is your translator? What is your source of power?" the tinny voice broke in once more. It seemed to come from a box on the side of the glass bowl worn by one of the afancs.

Kedrigern bit his lip and took a deep breath to calm himself. This was pushiness to an intolerable degree. To anticipate the summons of a wizard, to land this great white basin on his meadow in the precise spot where it would obstruct his favorite view, and then to interrupt him repeatedly with stupid questions about machines and strictly personal matters like his source of power, could be tolerated no longer. Kedrigern took a step back and extended his hand toward the afanc that had spoken. One good scorching blast of magic would do more to teach the thing manners than all the shouting Kedrigern could do in an afternoon.

As he lowered his hand, the afancs quickly reacted. Each of them drew from its side a silvery rod and pointed it at the wizard. Kedrigern spoke the word of power, and there was a tremendous crackle and zap, a sheet of light that broke into writhing ribbons, and a pungent smell in the air.

Rubbing at the spots that danced before his eyes, Kedrigern saw the afancs standing on the ramp as before. Nothing seemed to have happened to them. The silver rods were glowing brightly, dripping molten metal on the ground, where it struck with a spit and a hiss. The uneasy thought came to him that these afancs had some powerful magic behind them. The tinny voice, sounding a bit livelier, interrupted his rumination.

"This being has a powerful technology at his command. Never before has an organic life-form withstood the plasma beam," it said.

An identical tinny voice from its companion added, "Its shielding device would appear to be superior to our own. Notice the effect it had on the projectors. They are destroyed."

The two of them turned to face him. Though he was still a bit bedazzled by the brilliance of the flash, Kedrigern knew he must remain on the offensive. He hardened his expression and said, "Some damage has been done to my meadow. You will repair it before I release you."

"Release? Release?" both voices said at once, in a tone of querulous, metallic alarm. "We are not prisoners. You are prisoner."

"As you very well know, I brought you here to do a task for me. You're a bit ahead of time, but it's still a result of my summons, and you'd be wise not to forget that," said Kedrigern with forced calm. "When the task is completed to my satisfaction, I will release you from the spell and send you back where you came from. If you fail me, or try any more of these tricks, I will work another spell and send you someplace very nasty, and keep you there for a long, long time. Do you understand?"

"Do you claim that you brought us here?" one afanc asked.

"Of course. Now, since we will be working together, let us have no more talk of 'prisoners.' I'm willing to overlook your little prank, as long as you get to work and do the job properly. Here's the problem: Troam of the Terrible Temper had the poor judgment to make an insulting remark about Adajeva, a sorceress, and she—"

"Guidance system does not permit override by extravehicular agencies," one afanc broke in.

"I'm sure it doesn't," said Kedrigern condescendingly. "As I was saying, Adajeva learned of the remark and, understandably, she felt that she—"

"Your detectable power sources are insufficient to enable you to interfere significantly with our functions," the other afanc interrupted.

Kedrigern's expression became grim. "All right," he said softly. "That's it. I tried to be nice. I was ready to forgive and forget. But there will be no more carrot-and-stick for you two. Only stick, and I mean to lay it on hard!"

"The situation justifies use of the main plasma beam battery," said one afanc, and the other said, "Agree. Prepare main battery."

The huge white bowl spun, though its legs remained in place. A hole opened in its side. A group of large silvery rods emerged and turned to point at the wizard. He took the precaution of invoking a backup for his protective spell, and as the silvery rods locked on him, he closed his eyes tightly and clapped a hand over them as an extra precaution against the brilliant light that these creatures used in such an annoying way. The crackle and zap were much louder this time, the air tingled more palpably, and the smell was sharper. It was powerful magic, but it was unimaginative; merely repeating oneself on a larger scale, like shouting a repetition of some spell that had made no impression when simply spoken. It was typical of afancs: no finesse.

Kedrigern peeked between his fingers. The silvery rods looked like melted candles, and a charred patch encircled the hole from which they sagged. He felt very pleased with himself; it was always so satisfying to make the other fellow's magic work against him. Lowering his hand, he looked around and gave a cry of dismay at the sight of his meadow. It was black and smoking for a hundred paces in every direction.

"Now you're going to get it," he said with a swift gesture.

This time there were no rods to contend with, hence no noise and glare and stink. In an instant the afancs were each encased in a column of ice. That would hold them while the wizard decided on a suitable way to deal with them.

The voices sounded slightly muffled. There was a thin squeal to them as one said, "This is impossible," and the other, "Agree. This situation is incompatible with the laws of physics and cannot be occurring."

"If you think this is impossible, just wait," Kedrigern said ominously as he surveyed the blasted meadow.

"Yah, yah!" cried a distant voice. Spot burst from the house and bounded across the intervening space to its master's side, where it stopped, panting and salivating, eager to protect its master against the intruders.

"Thank you, Spot, but everything is under control now," the wizard reassured it, stooping to pat its warty head. "I'm just weighing my options for dealing with this pair!"

"Yah?" the little troll asked softly.

"If you like. Just don't touch the afancs. You might stick."

Kedrigern looked at the intruders, then at his blackened meadow, then at the afancs again. Should he simmer them slowly in a volcano? Freeze them solid and embed them in a glacier? Send them to the driest, sandiest waste in Araby? He weighed one form of chastisement against another, looked again at the meadow, and began to relent. A burn-off did the meadow no harm; in fact, it was beneficial. Everything would grow back next spring, probably greener than ever. All would be well, except for the afancs.

He looked thoughtfully upon the twin columns of ice. These wretched creatures could not help being what they were and acting as they did. Afancs will be afancs. They were dupes of some malicious intelligence, mere pawns, more sinned against than sinning. Severe and enduring punishment would be too cruel.

All the same, they needed a good lesson. They had been insufferably cheeky to a wizard, and such behavior could not be countenanced, or in a very short time every ogre, troll, fiend, goblin, and wicked fairy in the neighborhood would look upon him as Kedrigern the Soft, and make his life miserable with their pranks. Condign punishment was the thing, neither too lenient nor too severe, but just suited to the offense.

As Kedrigern stood in thought, scratching his chin and running through his inventory of punitive spells, Spot investigated the scene. It looked closely at the twin columns of ice, sniffing but not touching, in obedience to its master's command. Finding nothing of interest, Spot poked about in the blackened meadow, then turned its attention to the slender legs supporting the flying bowl. Sniffing revealed nothing, so Spot touched the thing gingerly. The base of the leg was a round pad about as thick as a man's forearm and perhaps three times as broad in diameter, hard on top but flexible on the bottom so as to adapt to the contours of the surface on which it rested. Spot pushed a hand underneath the pad, and felt it yield. He poked one adamantine finger into the top, and dented the metal slightly. Murmuring a thoughtful "Yah," the little troll stared at the leg for a moment and then, decisively, took a solid grip and tore the pad loose.

The grating of metal set Kedrigern's teeth on edge. The entire bowl gave a shudder, and anxious cries issued from the ice columns. Spot carried the pad and its accompanying length of leg to the wizard, dropping it at his feet with an earthshaking thud.

"Yah," said the troll with quiet pride.

"Thank you, Spot."

"No more! Spare our vessel!" the afancs cried as one.

"Are you requesting or commanding?" Kedrigern asked.

After a brief pause, one of the voices said, "We are imploring."

"Ah. Good. That's an improvement. Spot, you stay here by me. Don't tear off anything else until I give the word."

"Yah."

"Release us and we will spare your planet. We will leave and never return," said a voice from the ice.

"Not so fast. There's a matter of a few fire demons to be wet down."

"What is fire demons?"

"Don't play dumb. Every afanc knows what a fire demon is."

"What is afanc?"

"Afanc is *you*. Wizard is *me*. And don't forget it."

"You have misapprehended. We are not afanc."

"Really? Tell me, what are you, then?"

"We are Josporoxomixiloxil. We are all-knowing and all-powerful. We are masters of Josporoxomix Prime and its adjacent worlds, explorers of the cosmos, voyagers among the stars, conquerors of the universe."

"You don't seem to be doing too well."

After an embarrassed pause, one of the voices said, "Even conquerors of the universe do not win them all."

That was a profound observation, but not of much relevance to the matter at hand. The entire exchange only confirmed what Kedrigern had known all along: afancs are impossible to deal with. Either they bluster and bully, or they tell whoppers. Still, this particular whopper had a kind of outrageous appeal; it was not your ordinary fib, or typical traveler's tall story. Kedrigern found it amusing, and decided to see how far the afancs would carry it.

"Tell me more about Jos . . . about this place you come from," he said.

"It is difficult to speak at length when completely encased in ice," one voice replied.

"I suppose it is. All right, I'll release your top half. But no tricks, or you'll end up in the center of an iceberg."

The upper portion of each ice column vanished instantaneously. The intruders exchanged a glance, and one said, "We misjudged in classifying these beings as primitives. Their technology is most advanced."

Kedrigern was not certain what they meant, but their tone was respectful and he had no wish to disillusion them. He acknowledged the statement with a careless shrug and said, "We muddle along well enough. A spell here, a spell there, and the work gets done. I believe you were going to tell me about Jospox . . . about your home."

"Josporoxomix is the center of the universe and seat of all knowledge. It is the fourth of seven planets in a binary system, five of which have been fully colonized. Of the remaining planets, one is a penal colony, the other a refuse dump. Ours is a crowded system, but since the perfection of the Hooxl Stardrive, we have been able . . ." the tinny voice began.

Kedrigern let the creature rattle on. It was all gibberish, but the performance was amusing. He did his best to maintain a serious expression, now and then nodding or raising his eyebrows to indicate agreement or wonder, and interjecting an occasional "Ah," or "I see," to attest to his engrossment in the monologue. He was willing to go along with the joke. But at last, as afancs were wont to do, the creature exceeded all license.

"Ours is a binary system," it said, "composed of a blue giant and a red dwarf rotating around one another in perfect stability. It is believed—"

"Now you go too far," said Kedrigern. "I happen to know a number of giants personally, and dozens of dwarfs, and if there's one thing they are not, it's compatible. Giants are loners, and dwarfs are worse. They can't even stand to have other dwarfs around, let alone a giant. Particularly a *blue* giant."

After a pause, the afanc said, "Nevertheless, our suns are a blue giant and a red dwarf."

Kedrigern gave a whoop of laughter. "Oh, they're your sons, are they? Congratulations! Tell me, which of you is the father of the blue giant and which of the red dwarf? Or are you father and mother?"

"You do not believe in our description of the Josporoxomix system," said one afanc.

"I do not. You were very plausible and amusing until you started going on about things you clearly don't understand. I have visited several giants and come to know them fairly well. It's difficult to get close to a dwarf, but I've learned what I could about them. The two are utterly incompatible," the wizard said dogmatically.

The afancs turned toward one another. Flashing lights inside the bowls covering their heads suggested a lively exchange, which Kedrigern could not hear. When the lights faded, one afanc said, "Your words suggest unanticipated danger to the Josporoxomix system. Please explain."

"This has gone far enough, I think. We're chatting away here while Troam burns, and we really ought to get down to business. What I want you to do is—"

"Please explain. Important. You must explain danger of instability," the voice broke in.

"Now just stop it," said the wizard angrily. "I've been very patient, but when you—"

"Explanation is essential. Explain fully the danger to Josporoxomix system," said the voice, and the other chimed in, "Explain! Explain immediately! Tell us all you know! The system must be preserved!" in a rising pitch that pained the wizard's ears. He commanded them to stop, threatening more and thicker ice, but the unremitting metallic voices went on without pause, growing louder and more piercing. The two figures, still locked in ice from the midpoint down, waved their multiple arms and fingers in a distracting manner and began to vibrate. Holes opened in the sides of the flying bowl, and from them issued a deeper voice demanding, "Tell us all you know of the danger to our system! Reveal all! Tell all! Explain all!"

Furious, Kedrigern raised his hands and cried, "Go back where you came from this instant!" and uttered words of great power.

Bowl and afancs vanished. Nothing remained but a burnt patch in the meadow, five circular impressions in the grass, two puddles, and the footpad torn loose by Spot.

"Yah?" the little troll asked.

"I lost my temper," Kedrigern muttered.

"Yah."

"I know, I know. I should have had them take care of the fire demons before I let them go. But they got me angry. That's the last time I have anything to do with afancs."

"Yah?"

"I'll get in touch with a nixie. That will do the job. Or maybe a sea nymph. Troam would probably prefer a sea nymph. They're pretty little things. But Troam probably isn't much concerned about looks at this point. Just wetness. I suppose the safest thing would be a long, drenching rain." He pondered that for a moment, then brightened. "Yes, rain. I can get us a bit while I'm at it, and clean up the meadow. Rain it is. Nice and quick and clean. I'll have Troam soaked to the skin within the hour," he said, rubbing his hands together briskly. "Why didn't I think of this in the first place? Simple methods are usually the best. Fooling around with afancs . . . nasty, pushy things . . . no manners at all . . . brutes . . . liars . . . all that rubbish about seven planets going around a blue giant and a red dwarf . . . nonsense, utter nonsense." He shook his head irritably, and looked down on the broken footpad. He gazed upon it for a time, frowning, then he looked up into the immensity of the sky.

"Yah?" Spot asked.

He nudged the footpad with the toe of his boot. "Get rid of this thing. I don't want to see it again." As Spot trudged off to bury the pad, Kedrigern looked up again into the limitless blue, and said very softly, "Afancs."

Then he turned, and with lowered head and pensive expression he made his way over the singed meadow toward the house and his workroom.

Field Trip

by Gordon Linzner

"You're missing my point, Joe!" For emphasis, Bob stretched his arms out as far as the wrist chains allowed. "Once you know what a particular so-called 'unidentified flying object' *is,* it's no longer unidentified! It's swamp gas, or a weather balloon, or the planet Venus—"

"Or a flying saucer," Joe, sitting opposite Bob, interrupted through clenched teeth. His own chains were keeping his fingernails a tantalizing half inch short of the itch on his left ankle.

"Or a flying saucer," Bob conceded with a sigh, leaning back against the metal bulkhead. Once again, he tried to pierce the murk that defined the circle of light focused on Joe and himself; once again, he only made his eyes hurt. "The point is," he continued, "it doesn't make sense to get bent out of shape over the stuff that's too far away to even tell what it is, because you don't *know* it's a threat. Even if it *is* a flying saucer, you don't know it's from outer space. It could be some experimental Earth ship. And even if it's an alien spaceship, you don't *know* that culture is hostile. And even if it *is* . . ."

Joe was already bent out of shape, trying to reach his ankle. He tried willing the fingernail to grow faster, based on a vague memory of low-gravity experiments regarding growth rates of hair and cuticles. "Did you go on like this when your dad was teaching you to drive? I'm surprised you found time to start the engine."

"At least *I've* got a driver's license. Where's yours?"

"An accident of birth, Bobster. I'll have mine in six months, and on the *first* try." Joe stretched his fingers again. Maybe the perspiration around his wrist manacle would let him slide that precious half inch forward. Though he'd thought a spaceship would be cooler, somehow. "So how come, in the three weeks you've had that license, your dad hasn't let you take the car out by yourself?" He flexed his knee as far as he could. Ahh! Success!

"What about tonight?" Bob retorted.

"I seem to recall keeping the shotgun seat warm. Your dad let you go because I was with you. He knows I'm the responsible one." Joe took in a sharp breath. The itch was relieved, but now he had a cramp in his left leg from twisting it into an unnatural position.

Bob snorted. "I guess that reputation's not going to hold up after tonight."

"*I* told you not to drive toward that light!" Wincing, Joe straightened his leg.

"Had to find out what it was, didn't I?"

A loud thrum reverberated off the metal walls. Bob and Joe glanced up into the shadows. A large, dark-orange form stood at the edge of the light circle. It leaned forward. The thrum echoed again.

"We're in trouble now," Joe whispered, his cramp forgotten.

"This is a perfect example of what I'm talking about," Bob responded smugly.

"How does that cow-shaped thing with tentacles explain anything?" Joe asked.

"If you weren't chained down, you'd be looking for a hiding place right now. Am I right? Am I?" Bob smirked.

"Doesn't mean I'm chicken."

"Did I say that? Have I ever said that? Have I ever even *implied* that?"

The creature thrummed again, louder, and stamped its right front hoof.

"Implied, maybe," Joe replied.

Bob's chain rattled as he shook his head. "As usual, Joe, you hear what you want to hear, not what I'm saying. Look, we don't know what, or who, that creature is, right?"

"Pretty obvious to me that Bossie here is behind our abduction." The cramp became evident again, less painful but enough so as to add to Joe's irritability.

"On what evidence? He could be another prisoner."

Joe rattled his own restraints. "No chains, Bob. And it looks pretty ticked off."

"Of course! If you had a nice little cell all to yourself, and somebody threw in a couple of weird-looking aliens, wouldn't you be peeved?"

"You sound pretty convinced of your theory, Bob," Joe said slyly. "Not very open-minded of you."

"I didn't say that *isn't* our abductor, only that it might not be."

The creature stomped all four of its hooves in rapid succession, then turned and disappeared into the shadows.

"There!" said Joe triumphantly. "See? He's got the run of the ship. Would a captive be granted such privileges?"

"He might," Bob answered. "Like a prison trustee. Or that could be an alien pet. Ow!"

Bob's head banged the bulkhead behind him as the ship suddenly lurched, momentarily shifting the gravity field. Joe's body wrenched forward, then relaxed.

"Bang your head, Bob?" Joe asked.

"Obviously," came the sour response.

"It's not obvious to me. Maybe you only *thought* you banged your head. Maybe some weird alien probe was left in your brain when they examined us."

Bob patted his skull gingerly. "We weren't examined, just chained up. Remember?"

Gotcha! Joe thought. "That's the point, Bob. Our memories *could* have been altered."

"Now you're getting silly!"

"Just keeping our options open. Isn't that your argument? If we don't know something for sure . . ."

"You want options? I'll give you an option . . ."

None too gently, Barzk dumped the last two acquisitions near their primitive vehicle. It seemed a waste of fuel to return those chattering beasts to their homeworld, rather than simply space them. It wasn't as if they were likely to shut up long enough to breed. Unfortunately, Interstellar Conservation Laws were strictly enforced in this quadrant.

At least expenses could be written off. No one viewing the observation tapes could believe visitors to the Interstellar Preserve would pay to see such noisy, boring creatures more than once.

Though a temporary profit might have been made by charging an *exit* fee!

THE BOY, THE DOG, AND THE SPACESHIP

by Nicholas Fisk

There was a boy and his dog, running and rolling and chasing in a field.

There was a spaceship hurtling through nothingness, most of its crew already dead, and the rest despairingly fighting on to make landfall on a strange planet.

The boy's name was Billy. He was nine. His dog was called Scamp. He was young, too. Boy and dog understood each other perfectly.

Billy shouted, "Devil dog!" and pounced at Scamp. Scamp rolled his eyes, yelped with delight, and pranced off sideways. Billy chased Scamp until he was tired out. Then they sat down together, side by side in the evening shadows. When they had got their breath back, Billy shouted "Devil dog!" and the chase started all over again.

In the spaceship, the Captain contacted the Engineer. The channel was live—the Captain could hear the slight echoing hiss from the speaker. Or was it the Engineer's labored breathing?

The Captain barked, "Report. I want your report. Make your report."

The Engineer's breathing changed. It turned into long sobs. *"Report."*

The Engineer spoke. "It's no good, Captain, it's no good . . . ! The heat's burned out the bounce beam, the retros have gone dead. We'll just hit, Captain. We're going to smash."

Seconds later, the retros bellowed and the ship checked so violently that the Captain fell over. He got up bleeding. He said, "Engineer!" then noticed the Engineer's light had died, which meant that the Engineer had died. So he called the In-Flight Tech.

"In-Flight, we have full retro, am I correct?"

"Eighty percent retro, Captain. No more to come. But it may be enough—"

"It must be enough."

"Yes, Captain."

"Very well. Crashball, In-Flight. And tell the others."

"The others," the Captain said to himself. "Just two others . . ."

He switched off and began to fit himself into the crashball cocoon. He fitted webbing harnesses over his body and buckled them. He pressed a button and padded arms enfolded him. A little tubular snake leapt from a padded hole and latched itself to a socket near his neck; his clothing began to swell, then the walls of the cocoon. The puffed surfaces met. Now, he was completely encased in a puffy softness, pressing tighter and tighter.

He waited for the stab. It came. The needle darted itself into one of the Captain's veins. A drug entered his bloodstream. Almost immediately he felt drowsy and comfortable, but still alert. The same needle was connected to a whole junction of tiny tubes filled with his own blood and plasma; with stimulants, pain-killers, curatives and other life givers and life adjusters; even with painless death.

"Check in," said the Captain.

The In-Flight Tech and the Coordinator should have answered. Their lights were live. The Coordinator said, "Excuse me, Captain, but I think I'm dying." A moment later, he died.

"In-Flight Tech," said the Captain.

No answer.

"In-Flight Tech! Check in!"

"Yes, Captain?"

"Just checking," said the Captain, and switched off so that the Tech should not hear his sigh of relief.

The ship hurtled on. It was still slowing; the Captain could feel it through the cocoon. In the control center, the screens showed a green and blue planet with seas and clouds and land masses, coming nearer all the time. But there was no one outside the cocoons to watch the screens.

The boy whistled for the dog. "Here, boy!" he commanded and whistled again. "Come on, Scamp!"

Scamp pranced and curvetted toward the boy, being silly. He wanted to make the boy laugh, but the boy was solemn. He was proud of having such a well-trained dog. "Good boy," he said gravely. "Good old Scamp."

A minute later, the boy and the dog were wrestling in the grass.

* * *

The ship entered Earth's atmosphere. Its metal skin now drove against air instead of nothingness. The ship screamed. Its metal skin changed color and in places glowed dull red with the heat.

The In-Flight Tech's cocoon shifted, tearing from its framing. A cluster of tiny tubes pulled away from a socket, away from the needle. Blood, drugs, squirted uselessly. The In-Flight Tech died without a word.

The Captain watched his light go out and said, "All right. All right. Alone. I'll do it alone."

They stopped their wrestling match and looked about them.

"You heard it! It went sort of *wheeeoosh,*" Billy said to Scamp. "*Wheeeeooooosh.*" Scamp flicked his head sideways to acknowledge his master's words, but went on staring at the dark corner of the trees. Scamp had heard the noise. He didn't know where it came from, but he knew where it led. He marked the place in his nose and mind. Over there, by the dark trees.

"So that's what it's like," said the Captain. He had never before experienced a smash landing. He had to say something, even if there was no one to hear him. He kept his voice level.

He waited for the needle to deliver whatever his body needed. While he waited, he disciplined his mind and made it think and plan.

"Conquest," his mind said. "I am alone, but I am still here as a conqueror. I will conquer this planet.

"Method," he continued. "I am alone; but usual procedure will be followed. I will find a creature of the planet. I will invade its mind: make it obey me. I will then make all creatures of its kind obey the creature I inhabit.

"Having conquered one creature and one species, I will move on, always seeking the higher creatures. If there is a ruling species on this planet, I will invade a creature of that species and thus become ruler of all."

He pressed the release control. The halves of the cocoon opened.

The new conqueror of the planet Earth flexed his limbs, tested his organs and senses, opened the main doors, and stepped forth.

Billy pretended not to hear his mother's call, but then decided to obey. A long way away, right at the edge of the field, he could see the yellow glimmer of the lamp on her bicycle. "Uh, oh," he thought, "she's had to get on the bike to come after me. She won't be pleased . . ." To the dog he said, "Come on, Scamp. Come on, boy!" But Scamp was running back and forth by the dark trees.

"Bill-eeeee!" his mother shouted. "You come home now, or I'll—"

"It's Scamp, *he* won't come!" shouted Billy furiously.

And he wouldn't. Billy could see Scamp running up and down, doing a sort of sentry duty on the trot by the edge of the trees. The dog's ears were pricked, his tail was high, his body alert. He wouldn't obey.

* * *

The Captain's helmet indicators read SAFE, so the planet's air was breathable. Nevertheless, he kept his helmet on. He was glad to be protected with helmet and armor. He was grateful to the brains and skills that had designed his armored suit and given him a strength greater than his own. The Captain would clench a hand—and the suit's own metal hand would clench with such force that it could crush metal. The Captain was strong and fit—but his suit was tireless and inexhaustible. If the Captain's nerves, muscles, and movements said "run," the suit would run endlessly. If the Captain's body said "climb," the suit would keep climbing for him.

Now was the time, the Captain realized, to climb.

He had seen many worlds, explored many planets. He had never seen one like this. The world was bursting with life. From the corner of his eye, the Captain saw something move, very fast, on several legs. Above him, something flew. Behind him, something scurried. He was not in the least surprised. How could there fail to be active, animal life in so rich a place?

Climbing was what mattered now. He had to get on and up. Where he stood, he was completely surrounded and blinded by vegetable richness. Great green ribbed things, taller than the highest mountains of his own planet, reached indefinitely upward—no, not indefinitely, he could see dark blue sky still further above. A vast green trunk sprang from the soil very near him. It was the right size and shape, and it had projections: ideal for climbing. He clasped his limbs around this trunk. The suit took over and climbed him toward the dark blue sky, away from the ship with its hideous cargo of broken bodies; and from the stench of death.

At first there had just been a faint whiff of it. Now, it was a full-bodied and glorious stench—better still, a new stench! Scamp's black nostrils widened still further. There! Over there! He gave a stifled yelp of ecstasy as the smell strengthened; he bounded toward it.

"Billy!" said his mother. "Never mind the dog, you come home and eat your supper. Come on, now! I'm not waiting a moment longer!"

Billy stopped and gave one last yell. "Scamp! Scaaaaamp!"

Scamp did not hear. Only tracking down the smell mattered.

The Captain could climb no higher. The green column that supported him was bending and swaying under his weight. He wrapped his limbs around the column and felt the suit lock itself securely into position. He looked around him.

He was in a dense forest of green columns, all very much the same as the one he had climbed, yet each different. A few were rod-like (his column was ribbed and almost flat). Some columns carried grotesque explosions of strange branching shapes on their heads. A great nest of columns in the distance supported flat, outward-branching green platforms and—amazing!—complicated crown-shaped yellow platforms at their summits.

He adjusted his helmet to take in air from the outside. The air was moist, perfumed, sumptuous. He let the helmet supply his mouth with a sample of the moisture that was making droplets over everything; the water was cold, clean, simple, almost certainly safe—and absolutely delicious. On his own planet, he had tasted such air and water only in laboratories. Reluctantly, he returned to the closed-circuit environment of his suit and helmet . . .

An amazing planet! A planet of limitless, unending, inexhaustible richness! And he was to be its conqueror. The thought was stunning. For once, the Captain allowed himself simply to feel pleasure: to stare at nothing and to dream of glory.

Here! Scamp's nose was actually touching the wonderful source of the supreme stench!

He licked the source of the smell. It was cold and dewy and hard. He had expected something still warm, still half alive, still rubbery-soft; it was that sort of smell. But perhaps the cold, hard outer case was only a container, like the tube of bone that encloses the marrow? Carefully, he opened his mouth and picked up the container thing in his jaws. Nothing happened, so he put it down again, holding it between his front paws, and looked at it with his head on one side.

It seemed harmless. He lowered his head, opened his jaws, and bit.

The Captain saw a monster.

Once the terror and shock were over, there were

three things to be done (Past, Present, and Future, as the training manuals put it). First, understand exactly what had happened—the Past; second, make up your mind what immediate action to take—Present; third, decide what advantage could be gained by further action—Future.

All right. Past. He had seen the monster—a living thing, not a machine—travel at incredible speed, crash through the green columns and spires, trampling them flat in its haste. The monster was white, brown, and black and ran on legs. It had made straight for the crashed ship. When the monster's face opened, it was pink inside and had pointed white mountains above and below.

The monster had done various things, that the Captain could not see, to the ship. Finally it had picked up the ship, holding it between the white mountains, and crushed it. The Captain had heard the metal screech.

All right. Now the Present.

The body of the monster must be entered by the Captain so that the Captain could take it over in the usual way. He had to get nearer the monster. That should be easy enough provided that the monster did not suddenly go away on its big legs.

Finally, the Future.

Well, that was obvious enough, thought the Captain. Follow the normal procedure. Invade the monster's brain and gain control of its body and its actions.

After that, the invasion would follow its normal course. All species—high or low—would eventually obey the Captain. By then, the Captain would have contacted his home planet. More ships would come bearing settlers. At last the Captain would have found a safe, fitting, rich, and permanent home.

He went toward the monster.

Billy picked at his supper, but his mother said, "Do eat up!" and watched him until he finished every morsel. He didn't want food. He wanted Scamp.

His mother said, "And do your homework." She bustled out of the room. A minute or so later, he heard the TV. She liked that program; she never missed it! And she wouldn't miss *him*.

He tiptoed to the back door, opened it silently, closed it silently, and was on his way to the big field.

The Captain was within reach. The white parts of the monster glowed pale but clear in the failing light. The Captain muttered, "Climb." The suit took him up fast.

The Captain had chosen a green spire to climb—a flat-sided spire that would bend when he reached the top of it. The monster was not moving. It was crouched over the remains of the ship. "Climb. Climb . . ."

Just as he reached the right place and was about to sway the tip of his spire toward the monster, the monster moved! The Captain made a split-second decision and leaped into nothingness. He stretched his limbs—clutched—and held. Victory!

Gripping one cluster of white or brown or black rods after another, the Captain clambered his way along the monster, making for the brain. It was above the monster's face. He could feel the brain's energy.

He came to the entrance of a tunnel leading into the monster's head and smiled. He clambered into the tunnel, the suit making light work of the journey. Now the brain signals were deafening—even the helmet was overwhelmed. The Captain turned back. He made himself comfortable outside the entrance of the tunnel, anchoring himself securely. He checked some readings and responses. Good. The monster was hearing him.

"You'll enjoy this," the Captain told the monster. "You'll like obeying me. You'll like the things we do. You *will* obey me, won't you? Of course you will. You *will* obey me, always . . ."

Billy found Scamp. At first he was glad to find him, but soon he was puzzled. Scamp kept shaking his head, and he was running. "He's got a burr in his ear," thought Billy. "Or an insect. An itch."

Scamp was running in regular patterns—a straight line, a pause, a turn to the left, then another straight line, then a pause and a turn to the right. It looked weird in the moonlight. Billy began to be frightened.

Then Scamp suddenly sat down, some ten yards away, and looked straight at Billy. The dog did not move a muscle. He just stared.

The Captain halted the monster—the up-and-down motion of the monster's running disturbed his thought—and thought very carefully.

"The monster is a servant creature," he decided. "And the upright monster, the one that just arrived, is a superior creature because he makes audio signals and expects them to be obeyed. How do I know that? Because when the upright monster made his signals, my monster was uneasy. He tried to disobey me." The Captain smiled a little at the thought.

"But does it matter which monster is the master?" he thought. Probably not. They are both much the same size. If they fought, who knows which would win?

"Not that *that* matters much either," thought the Captain. "Because I am the controlling brain. So I could appoint either as the master species of the planet. Nevertheless . . ."

Billy shouted, "Scamp! Come here when I call you!" But Scamp just sat there in the moonlight, staring straight at him, motionless.

Billy said—this time almost pleading—"Come on, boy. Good boy. Come on, Scamp. Please."

But the dog just stared, and his eyes looked strange in the moonlight.

"Nevertheless," thought the Captain, "it might be as well to find out which is master. Besides, one or other of them might have powerful weapons I should know about. I'll try it."

He spoke to the dog's brain.

"Kill," said the Captain. "Kill that other creature there."

* * *

The dog attacked. "Scamp!" yelled Billy. "Don't, Scamp!"

Scamp overran him and turned and charged again, snarling like a hound of hell. And then the dog had hurtled the boy to the ground and was standing over him, jaws open, teeth bared.

"Scamp!" It was a scream of terror. The dog paused. The big voice in his head said, *"Kill!"* but the old, loved familiar voice was calling, too, asking for help.

The dog paused; the boy struck out blindly with his fist. He hit the dog's ear. Something small fell to the ground unseen. The little thing was mortally wounded. It writhed.

Scamp said, "Whoof!" in a vague way and looked at Billy. The dog licked the boy's face, wagged his tail, and sheepishly got off Billy's chest. He sat down and scratched his ear with a hind paw. But the itching had gone.

The little, unseen thing writhed for the last time; and, hidden in the grass, the Captain died.

The boy and the dog rollicked off together across the moonlit field. Sometimes the boy chased the dog; sometimes the dog chased the boy. When they got home, they were both scolded by Billy's mother.

By the edge of the trees, the dew was heavy on the spaceship. Soon it would rust and become as brown as the earth. But now it was still shiny and glinting in the tall weeds. In the moonlight, you wouldn't have noticed where its body was crushed and dented. It looked like a super-perfect model. Little, but marvelously made.

FIREFLIES

by Nancy Etchemendy

Spencer had never seen so many fireflies in one place before, or seen them so large or so bright. Beyond the kitchen window, the woods behind the house looked like Christmas at the mall. The dancing lights were big for fireflies—nearly the size of a fingertip. An eerie, faint whine a little like bumblebees, a little like wasps, drifted through the screen. He had never heard fireflies make a sound like that. A shiver skittered across his shoulders, quick as a wild mouse. He wanted to take a closer look.

He knew his mother wouldn't approve if he tried to catch one. But not just because these were different and maybe a little scary—she had moral objections to the whole idea of catching bugs.

"How would you like it if a big, mean giant put you in a jar and stared at you till you got so exhausted you stopped moving?" That's what she'd said the last time he came in with a jar full of dragonflies and moths.

But how could he resist? His parents weren't home. They had gone for an evening walk, and left him to baby-sit his three-year-old sister, Melina. What could it hurt? He would put a few of the fireflies in a jar, watch them for a minute or two, then set them free before his mom and dad got home. Nobody would ever have to know a thing about it.

He used the stepladder in the pantry to climb to the top shelf where his mom stored the empty jars. There were all kinds. He recognized them by their shapes, even though the labels were gone. Some had once held mayonnaise, some had held dill pickles or berry jam. A lot of them had once held Spiffy peanut butter. Spiffy was about the only thing Melina would eat, and she ate tons of it. His parents made special trips to World O' Food to buy it by the case, in the largest possible size.

Spiffy jars were perfect for fireflies. They had good, wide mouths, and they were made of clear plastic so they never broke, even if you dropped them. He grabbed one and hurried back into the kitchen, thinking about ways to punch holes in the lid. Meanwhile, the fireflies danced and darted beyond the window, and the humming got a little louder.

As he walked past the kitchen table, Melina jumped out from under it and clamped herself around his right leg.

"Gaaahhh!" he shouted. He tried to shake her off, but it would have been easier to shake his own foot off. The family's golden retriever, Phreeto, who hated to be left out of anything that looked like a game, rushed over and clamped himself joyfully around Spencer's other leg.

"Gaaahhh! Gaaahhh!" shouted Spencer. No other word quite captured the way he felt. Baby-sitting Melina was always like this. When he told his parents he would rather clean up dog doo than baby-sit, they usually just smiled and said they knew she was "active," but he could handle it. Active? Right. He wondered if they would call a shark or a band of South American natives with blowguns "active."

"Wanna Spiffy samwich!" Melina yelled.

Phreeto howled and licked Spencer's hand.

Spencer clomped around the kitchen, shaking his legs and shouting, "Get off! Get off! Can't you see I'm busy right now?"

"Make me a samwich!" said Melina.

He took a deep breath and forced himself to stand still a moment. He squinted at Melina in a way he hoped would look ominous. "All right. I'll make you a sandwich. But first you have to say 'please.' And you have to promise you'll let go of my leg and you'll be good for the rest of the night. You have to promise something else, too."

"What?" said Melina.

"You have to promise to keep a secret."

He felt her grip loosen ever so slightly. She was interested. "What secret?"

"We're going to catch fireflies. But we won't do it, and you won't get your sandwich, unless you promise not to tell anybody. Ever."

Phreeto sat down and wagged his tail. Melina pressed her lips together hard. After a couple of seconds she said, "Okay. Please." She let go of his leg.

Melina's bare feet smacked the linoleum behind him as he walked over to the counter and got out a butter knife and a half-full jar of Spiffy.

"Happy peanut," said Melina. She touched the Spiffy logo on the label, a cartoon drawing of a peanut with legs and a smiling face.

"Yeah, happy peanut," said Spencer, not paying much attention. He spread two slices of bread thickly with peanut butter while he stared through the window at the insect light show outside.

He handed Melina the sandwich without looking at her, then hurried to the other end of the counter, where he knew there was an ice pick in a drawer. The ice pick was his tool of choice for making holes in jar lids. But it took a minute to find it among the measuring spoons, can openers, tangles of string, and other junk that littered the drawer.

He had just picked it up when he heard a funny squeak. He turned to see what it was, and discovered Melina standing on the counter, using both hands to finger-paint the window with peanut butter. Her face and clothes were smeared with it. On the floor, Phreeto chomped down the remains of her sandwich.

"Me-LI-naaaa!" Spencer yelled. "What are you doing? What a mess. We're gonna be bug meat when Mom and Dad see this!"

But Melina didn't seem to be listening. She leaned against the window, palms braced on the glass, and lifted one hand.

"Look," she said, her voice whispery with wonder. "They're pretty."

Dozens of fireflies had arranged themselves on the outside of the window in the softly glowing shape of Melina's hand. Spencer watched them, his mouth half open. Some of them were as big as lemon drops, and nearly as round. He had never seen fireflies that looked like these, and he had never seen them do anything like this. He had never even heard of it. For a long moment, it seemed as if the only sounds in the world were the distant ticking of the clock in the living room, the bee-like buzz of whatever they were, and the slow whump of his own heart.

"I'm going outside," he said slowly. He felt as if he might be dreaming.

"Me, too," said Melina.

Spencer didn't hear her. He was too busy punching holes in the jar lid.

The screen door groaned as he swung it open and stepped into the eerie dusk. The air was thick with bobbing, greenish lights. The leaves of his mother's rosebushes drooped with them. One buzzed around his ears, then another. He felt a stickery sensation as one landed on the back of his neck. He batted at it, and it flew off, whining angrily. Half a dozen settled on the front of his T-shirt. He dropped the jar. It bounced on the flagstone path as he swatted at the bugs with both hands, breathing hard, beginning to sweat a little.

Behind him, Melina gave a long, high-pitched scream that stopped suddenly.

He whirled around. When he saw Melina, he would have screamed, too, except he couldn't catch his breath. If he hadn't known who and what she was, he wouldn't have recognized her. Every inch of her was covered with glowing, jostling bugs. She stood completely still—much too still for a normal three-year-old. She looked like a neon garden statue. On the other side of the screen door, Phreeto barked the way he did whenever he was terrified by thunder or a stranger whose smell he didn't trust.

Three of the bugs had landed on the back of Spencer's hand, right in a glob of Spiffy peanut butter. Trembling, he looked as closely as he dared. They were shaped like slightly flattened spheres. No matter how hard he stared, he couldn't see any wings. They didn't seem to have any eyes, either, though a line of shiny dark spots ringed each glowing body. He had seen a lot of bugs in his life, but he had never come across one with eyes like these, if that's what they were.

The bugs reminded him of something, but he couldn't quite think what it was.

He told himself to wake up. Nothing happened, except he noticed that his skin became tingly and numb where the fireflies touched it. He felt like shaking his hand wildly so they would be flung far away from him and he wouldn't have to think about them anymore. But part of him knew that might be a big mistake. What if they were like wasps? When you made wasps mad, they stung and called for reinforcements. And even if he got all the bugs off himself, what about Melina?

He edged closer to her. There were so many fireflies on her that he couldn't see her skin. Even her eyelids were covered with them.

He held his hands and arms out in front of him and studied them. He gazed down at his T-shirt and his legs encased in blue jeans. There weren't nearly as many fireflies on him as there were on Melina—just a few clusters here and there in no particular pattern. But why? He couldn't think of any good reason.

"What do you want?" he shouted at the darting lights among the trees, on the rosebushes, hovering above the lawn, crowding over his sister's small body.

As if in answer, a stream of fireflies poured toward him from the woods and the garden. He dropped back a couple of steps, ready to run. But they stopped three or four feet in front of him. Shifting patterns took shape as they moved around each other in midair. They made Spencer think of a marching band on a football field, building a picture with their bodies. But what was it?

A lump. Straight lines. Two dots and a curve like a smiley mouth. Suddenly, Spencer could see the whole shape hanging in the fragrant twilight air like a buzzing hotel sign. He would have laughed if he hadn't been so terrified. It was a peanut with legs and a happy face. The Spiffy logo!

All at once, Spencer understood. The bugs were clustered on him exactly in the places where he had accidentally gotten peanut butter on himself while fixing Melina's sandwich. They must have swarmed Melina because she was covered with it from head to toe. Heck, she ate so much Spiffy she was practically made of it.

With a jolt almost like an electric shock, he realized what the fireflies reminded him of. They weren't just flattened spheres. They were shaped like diminutive saucers. What if the eyes were windows? What if the humming, which had never sounded quite right for insects, was really the whine of tiny engines? Who said UFOs had to be gigantic!

He sprinted toward the house before he quite knew what he was going to do. He found himself flinging open the pantry door and pulling out his mom's entire supply of Spiffy, twelve extralarge jars in a big cardboard box. It must have weighed thirty pounds, but he was so full of adrenaline that he lifted it as if it were a beachball. He ran back outside and tipped all the jars out onto the grass a few feet away from Melina, who hadn't moved a finger as far as he could tell.

One by one, he unscrewed all the tops and tore open the seals. The delicious aroma of fresh peanut butter drifted out across the garden. The Spiffy seemed to suck the miniature saucers toward it like a high-powered vacuum cleaner. Within two seconds, there was not a single one left on Spencer. Melina, bug-free at last, let out a howl of pure horror.

Spencer scooped her up and skidded through the doorway as if he were sliding into home plate. He slammed the front door and bolted it, then ran around to all the windows and did the same. Phreeto bounded after him, growling and barking as if to say, "Hurry! Faster!"

He and Melina watched through the kitchen window as their mother's mammoth Spiffy supply dwindled to nothing. It took about five minutes. Spencer blinked, just once. In that tick of time, the firefly saucers disappeared without a trace, making off like pirates with treasure, through invisible holes in space for all he knew.

He opened the door and stared out through the screen, which he kept tightly hooked. The empty jars were as spotless as if they had been run through a dishwasher. The night songs of crickets and frogs had replaced the unearthly whir of the tiny alien ships. He should have felt comforted, but he didn't.

Melina buried her face in his T-shirt and sobbed, "Bad Spiffy!"

Spencer ruffled her hair as he thought about the rest of the town—the children who might not have a ransom of peanut butter with which to buy their freedom, the unsuspecting adults out for walks.

He wished his parents would come home.

They'd been gone a lot longer than they'd said they would be.

Overseer

by Al Sarrantonio

"No, I tell you I'm on to something, Bill. You *have* to keep printing them!"

The voice on the other end of the line said something nasty.

"Oh, yeah? And the same to you!" Nathan Halpern slammed the wall phone back into its cradle. Instinctively he checked the coin return to see if anything had dropped into it. "Blast," he said, and walked back to the bar.

The bartender smiled. "Almost never works."

Halpern waved him off, taking a sip of his beer. "That's not what I'm mad about," he said. He pulled a crumpled newspaper clipping from the pocket of his equally rumpled sports jacket and pushed it across the bar. "Here," he said, "look at this."

It was a slow Wednesday afternoon in the Golden Spoon Tavern, in the dead center of a killing August heat wave. The lunch crowd, what little there was of it, had long gone, and besides Nathan Halpern the only other customers the bartender had to worry about were two regulars at the other end of the bar, each of whom, like clockwork, drank one scotch on the rocks every half-hour; and since it was nearly twenty minutes until the next round was due, the bartender could afford to socialize. He took the clipping and read:

FISH FALL FROM SKY

COPANAH, *NY (Aug. 12)*—Residents of the small town of Copanah, ten miles northeast of Albany, reported a rain of dead fish yesterday. The creatures, which resembled cod in appearance, were scattered over an area two miles square, and local residents insist that they dropped from the heavens.

One elderly resident of the town, Sam Driller, whose integrity was vouched for by several neighbors including Copanah's mayor, stated that he had gone out to move some trash cans to the street for pickup when "a whole barrelful of fish dropped right on top of me. I looked up, and the sky's full of 'em—they was dropping right out of the clouds. It ain't natural, but I swear I saw it."

Two local policemen and the daughter of the town librarian also witnessed the event, and local authorities could offer no explanation. A spokesman for Margolies Air Force Base, thirty miles away, reports that none of its aircraft were in the air at that time.

The bartender folded the clipping and handed it back to Halpern. "So?" he said. "Silly stuff like that turns up in the papers every summer." He cocked his head toward the telephone on the wall. "I heard part of your conversation. You wrote this?"

"Yeah." Halpern nodded glumly. "And you don't think there's anything to it either?"

The bartender drew Halpern another beer, setting it down in front of him. "That one's on the house. To tell you the truth, no."

Halpern leaned across the bar and tapped his finger against the wood. "I checked every one of those witnesses myself."

The bartender shrugged. "Doesn't mean a thing. All those people could easily have been lying."

Halpern nearly knocked his beer over. "No way!" he said excitedly. "I know it's supposed to be the dog days and all that, but this stuff is for real. I've checked it out. It goes on all the time all over the place. Little clusters of reports here, little clusters there. The only reason you see more stuff in the paper in July and August is because there's nothing else to print. But these things actually happen all the time, since before newspapers existed. And this time they're happening here in Albany County."

The bartender still looked skeptical.

"Look—" Halpern took a sip of beer and wiped his mouth with his sleeve "—have you ever heard of Charles Fort?"

The bartender scratched his head. "Wrote a bunch of paperbacks, right?"

Halpern nodded. "Something like that. Fort was a kind of journalist. Spent over twenty-five years in the New York Public Library and the British Museum collecting stories from newspapers and scientific journals—stories like the one I showed you. He had thousands and thousands of clippings and articles, and he put them into books like *Lo!* and *The Book of the Damned.* He documented all kinds of weird things—wolf children, devil sightings, flying saucers, volcanic eruptions spewing out human limbs instead of lava—you name it. He didn't take all of it seriously, but he was convinced that everything that happens is somehow *connected;* that there is only one unified reality that everything is tied to. One of his favorite quotes was, 'I think we're all property.' "

The bartender laughed. "We are," he said. "We're all owned by the IRS."

Halpern didn't smile. "Charles Fort was no nut. After he died back in the thirties, a bunch of people like Theodore Dreiser, Ben Hecht, and Alexander Woollcott got together and started the Fortean Society to continue the work he was doing. It still exists."

The half-hour chime sounded on the cuckoo clock over the cash register, and the bartender mixed and delivered two more scotches to the regulars. When he came back, he looked thoughtful.

"So you really think there's something behind it?"

Halpern nodded. "I've checked out too many of these stories to think they're all baloney. I swear there's a pattern to it all, just like Fort believed."

"Well, I'm still unconvinced. From what I've seen behind this bar, you can find patterns wherever you want to."

Halpern leaned close, and a conspiratorial tone came into his voice. "Do you know someone named Rita Gartenburg?"

"Sure," the bartender replied. "I've lived down the block from her for twenty years."

"She a drunk? Or a nut?"

"No way!" said the bartender. "Never seen her in here or any other gin mill in town. And she's no kook. She's a nice, steady lady who grows prize roses in her backyard."

"Well," said Halpern, "prize-winning or not, she told me she saw a bunch of those same rosebushes get up off the ground and walk around."

The bartender's jaw dropped. "You must be kidding."

"That's what she told me," said Halpern, "and that's the way I'm going to report it. She even took a couple of pictures, but the things didn't come out."

The bartender shrugged. "I don't know what to think."

Halpern downed his beer and prepared to leave. "You know," he said, "I used to be a hotshot columnist, weekdays *and* in the Sunday supplement. Political reporter." He shook his head. "But I never believed anything as strongly as I believe this stuff. I've been at it two months now, ever since the Fourth of July, when a bunch of kids near my house said they saw a skyrocket land back on the ground and run away." He gave a short laugh and held two fingers a quarter-inch apart as he backed through the door. "I'm telling you, there's something there, and I'm getting closer to it all the time."

**SKY GOES BLACK AT NOON
ON SUNNY DAY**

SUMPTERSVILLE, NY (Aug. 20)—According to residents of Sagerstown, four miles east of Sumptersville, the sky suddenly turned black at twelve noon yesterday. Local weather charts showed that the day was cloudless and sunny, with north-northwest winds at six to eight miles per hour, but an affidavit signed by nearly all of the seventy-six residents of the tiny community, known statewide for its annual cornbread festival each September, swore that at exactly twelve o'clock "the sky went completely dark, as if God Himself had pulled a light switch off."

There were no stars visible during the occurrence, which lasted approximately five minutes, and an eerie silence seemed to come over the town. Then suddenly, according to the statement, it was bright daylight again.

Witnesses and signers of the affidavit included six members of the local town council, as well as retired weatherman Jed Burns, who worked for local TV station WWWM for twenty-three years. Reached for comment, Burns said that he was "still in a stunned condition" and had no idea what had happened. He said he has tried to get the U.S. Weather Bureau involved in the matter, but that so far they have shown no interest.

"I tell you, Bill," Halpern yelled into the phone, "I'm real close!"

There was silence on the other end for a moment, and then a squawking sound that lasted for a minute and a half.

At the end of it, Halpern waited a few seconds. "No, Bill," he said calmly, "I have not been out in the sun too long. I've told you from the beginning of this thing that you should just let me run with it, and I'm telling you again. When I break it open, I'll come back to Albany and be a good boy."

There was another short squawk on the other end.

"That's right, a good boy. Cover the state legislature and everything. I promise. But you have to let me follow this through."

Another squawk.

"That's right. Six-headed chickens and all. But that was yesterday, editor mine. Today it was ball-point pens dropping through the ceiling of a supermarket."

Another squawk—actually, more of a screech this time, louder and more insistent.

"Didn't you hear me at all? I said I'm beginning to see a pattern to all this. This could be my chance to be Woodward and Bernstein, Bill."

Squawk.

"No, I haven't actually seen any of it. I always seem to be one town behind, and when I guess where the next thing will occur, I always guess wrong. But I'll break the code. And yes, the chicken *could* have been fake, but it wasn't. Believe me, it's beginning to click."

Silence on the other end; then a low, rasping sound.

"That's right, Bill—Woodward and Bernstein. Sure you got that whole story? Okay, call you tomorrow."

COW GIVES BIRTH TO TWO DOGS

POKERTON, NY (Aug. 23)—Bill Gainesborough, a small farmer in this dairy farming community,

> swears that one of his cows gave birth to two puppies earlier this week. Gainesborough, who was upset by the event and hesitant to talk about it to reporters, stated that his cow Ilse, one of thirty milk cows on the farm, gave birth to two dogs "right in front of my eyes."
>
> The puppies are cocker spaniels, and there are no cocker spaniel owners within ten miles of the Gainesborough property. Neighbors, who urged the farmer to talk about what had happened, swore that Gainesborough was not the kind of man to pull a hoax. The puppies were given to a local foundling home.

Halpern didn't call his editor back the next day. On Wednesday the twenty-fifth, he found himself in Lolarkin, where a group of schoolboys claimed to have seen three moons in the sky. Thursday the twenty-sixth found him in Crater, where two grandmothers and twelve of their kin swore that their house had lifted itself off its foundation, turned around 180 degrees, and set itself back down again. On Friday he was in Peach Hollow, just missing a rain of black tar. Saturday he spent in Cooperville, arriving a scant three minutes after two hamsters had talked in a crowded pet store; he'd guessed right on that location, but had miscalculated as to time. Sunday morning the twenty-ninth he sat in a diner in Reseda, staring at a horribly creased map of the state, when suddenly the pattern rose before his blurry eyes.

He shoved the map under his arm as he dialed the

phone. His hands were shaking. He stared back across the room at his eggs getting cold while the phone rang.

"Bill, it's me."

This time there wasn't squawking, but rather a high and steady whine.

"I *know* it's Sunday morning. No, I didn't know it was six o'clock. I've been up all night."

His hands wouldn't stop shaking.

"Shut up, Bill," he said into the phone as the whining started up again. He fumbled the map up to his eyes. "It's simple. Crisscross, crisscross. These things have been making little *x's* all over the county. And you know what that means? Something, some single source, is behind it all."

Silence.

"Did you hear me?"

Silence again. Then a carefully phrased question.

"No, I won't tell you where I am. Wait for me to phone in my story. But I'll bet you even money that I'm in the place where the next thing happens. Just another day or two, Bill. That's all I need."

Silence. Then a sigh.

"Thanks, Bill. If you were here I'd kiss your ugly face."

BOY TELEPORTED FROM OWN HOUSE TO NEIGHBOR'S

GRAFTON, NY (Aug. 30)—Ten-year-old Bobby Milestone, who vanished into thin air while playing quietly in his own front yard today, was found an hour later in the home of Grafton neighbor Mr.

> Fred Warbling. The youth claimed to remember nothing that happened to him between the time he vanished and reappeared. "I was out front one second," he stated, "and the next second I was on top of Mr. Warbling's car in his garage."
>
> The youth vanished before the startled eyes of his uncle, Mr. Eugene Milestone, who was looking out the window when the incident occurred. "It was like somebody yanked him out of the air," Mr. Milestone said.
>
> This reporter was on hand and participated in the massive hour-long search, which was mounted immediately after young Milestone vanished. No explanation has been offered for the youth's disappearance and subsequent reappearance.

Halpern called in the Milestone piece on Monday afternoon over Bill Greener's loud protestations. All the rest of the day he double- and triple-checked his calculations, readying himself for the next day's sighting. He rented a car and was on the road before nightfall, munching periodically on a bucket of fried chicken as he drove. Before leaving he sent a cable to Greener which read: I WAS RIGHT, YOU SUCKER. HAVE REACHED END OF SEARCH. WILL KNOW ALL TOMORROW. BRACE FOR BIG STORY.

He drove for four hours, pulling to a halt well before dawn at his calculated site. There was no moon and the visibility was bad, but he seemed to be on a road at the edge of a vast, rolling valley in the middle of nowhere. He shrugged and went to sleep for a couple of hours, awakening just as dawn broke. When he looked out the window, his eyes widened.

"My God," he gasped. "I was right."

There, a scant fifty yards off the dusty road, sat a machine. It looked like nothing so much as an airship, a dirigible-like structure with a long cabin slung underneath. It bore no identifiable markings.

As Halpern drew closer, he saw that his first impression had been a bit mistaken; the thing was not quite as rickety as it first appeared. It was smoothly metallic and resembled a conventional cigar-shaped flying saucer.

And as he crept even closer, he saw that there was a doorway in the cabin underneath, and a figure leaning against it with his arms folded. Just as Halpern reached the ship, the figure waved languidly and turned away, disappearing inside. Cautiously, Halpern poked his head through the opening—and heard someone say, in an even tone, "Please come in, Mr. Halpern."

He entered the craft, stepping as if he were walking on eggs.

Inside, the cabin was a cluttered mess; stacks of papers and charts lay everywhere. A man was at the front of the structure, bending over a control panel composed of antique knobs and a huge bronze steering wheel. Two globes, one celestial and one terrestrial, were mounted on either side.

The man turned, and Halpern at once thought he looked vaguely familiar. He was strongly built, taller than average, and bore a slight resemblance to Teddy Roosevelt, with a bushy mustache and curling hair parted a bit left of center. He wore a pince-nez, and

Halpern was at once taken with the calmness of the gray eyes behind it. He also wore a three-piece woolen suit with a watch-chain and fob attached.

"Please sit down, sir," the man said, indicating a camp stool off to the right. "I'll be with you in a moment." He turned to the control panel, and Halpern spun around to see the door to the craft closing with a smooth hiss. Moments later there was a nearly undetectable bump. They were airborne.

With a sigh the man turned from the control board and confronted Halpern with those calm gray eyes.

"I must congratulate you," he said, "on your perseverance. I was happy to see you'd found my little pattern. And that you were clever enough to notice that the last little *x* in my grid of *x's* would be completed today." The corners of his eyes wrinkled upward—in mirth or perhaps something else. "Very resourceful. You thought there might be something at the end of my rainbow of crisscrosses, eh?"

Halpern nodded cautiously.

The stranger suddenly thrust out his hand. "Well, you were right, of course. My name is Charles Fort, sir."

The man paused a moment to watch Halpern's jaw drop, then went on: "You've become something of a pest these last few weeks, you know. But I must say you've been an interesting pest." Once again his eyes seemed to twinkle.

"You *can't* be Charles Fort," said Halpern. "Fort died fifty years ago."

The other's eyebrows went up. "Did he? I suppose you need a bit of explanation, eh?"

Halpern said nothing.

"First of all," the man said, "I really am Charles Fort. Or was, anyway, for a time. Actually, you might call me a kind of 'overseer.' I was sent here to Earth a very long time ago, Mr. Halpern. My life here as Charles Fort, from 1874 to 1932, was an enjoyable sidelight to my real task, and so to amuse myself I decided to document some of my own doings."

Halpern's eyes widened. "You mean *you* made all the strange things happen? The trees flying around, the puppies—all that?"

Fort smiled modestly. "That's right. Beautifully ironic, isn't it? That Charles Fort not only documented all sorts of bizarre phenomena, but actually *caused* them all!" Laughing, he gestured toward the controls. "I do it all with these little knobs. Flying frogs, double suns, night for day, day for night, invisibility—all the silly stuff."

"I can't believe it!" said Halpern. "*Why?*"

Fort's laugh ended in a sigh. "Well," he said, "I've been here a very long time. Doing a job." He yawned, then glanced behind him out of the port windows, pushing at the rudder wheel a fraction. "Not a very exciting one, I'm afraid. Let's just say my job was to start things rolling on this planet, as far as civilization was concerned, and then to—" A hint of a smile touched his lips. "—help things along, so to speak. *Not* to interfere," he added hastily, "but rather to keep you moving, evolving, keep you on your toes. We're not allowed to interfere directly, you know." He smiled dreamily, fingering his lapel. "I always liked the clothes from the turn of the century best."

Halpern was getting impatient. "But why did you invent Charles Fort?"

"Boredom, Mr. Halpern. Flying around in this ship all the time, causing mischief here and there—it all gets exceedingly tiring. So I decided to live among you for a while. I made up a being named Charles Fort. Gave him birth records, a family history, everything he needed. Granted, I was bending the rules a bit. But if all I did was chronicle my own doings, I wasn't *directly* interfering, was I? And my job at the same time—doubly so, since I was not only perpetrating all those 'unexplained phenomena,' but bringing them to your attention at the same time. As I said, beautifully ironic."

"But what's all this 'overseer' stuff? You mean to say you came here just to play tricks on us?"

Fort sighed heavily. "For better or for worse, Mr. Halpern, somebody a long time ago decided that this was the way to bring young civilizations along. The object is, quite simply, to make you *think.* To make you look at the world as a strange and beautiful place with mysteries still not fathomed—which, of course, it is." He gave the rudder another touch. "And the more you wonder about what's behind this weird, wonderful universe you live in, sooner or later you'll begin to realize that everything is rather neatly tied together—that it's all a unity. And the sooner you come to understand that unity, the sooner you can, well, join the club, so to speak. While I was Charles Fort down below I cheated a little by sneaking some of that monistic philosophy into my books. But what's a little cheating in a good cause, eh?" He smiled. "So you see, all my hijinks are really just a teaching tool." Suddenly he came over to Halpern and put his arm around his shoulder. "I bet you can't *wait* to get back and tell your story, eh?"

"Yes . . ." said Halpern cautiously.

"Well, you must let me show you a few of my little tricks first, and then we'll get you back to your office, safe and sound. You see, I *know* what it's like to be a newspaperman."

Once more the limpid gray pools of Fort's eyes sparkled as he led Halpern toward the back of the airship.

"I have a little confession to make," he said, smiling paternally. "You're the first human being I ever let catch me in the act. That's *really* bending the rules, isn't it? But since I'm getting you back to your office, I guess I'm not interfering all that much."

"Sure, why not?" said Halpern, suddenly buoyant, thoughts straying once again to Woodward and Bernstein. He laughed. "That really was a clever line of yours, by the way. 'I think we're all property.' Very clever."

"It was at that, wasn't it?" Fort smiled.

VIOLENT INCIDENT AT DATA TERMINAL

ALBANY COMPLEX, NY (Aug. 31, 2082)—An intruder dressed in pre-Millennium clothes and claiming to be an employee of the *Albany Sun* caused minor damage at this station's mid-Complex terminal earlier today. The man, who identified himself as Nathan Halpern, stated in loud terms that he was a top *Sun* "columnist," demanded a "typewriter" (such devices have not been used at the *Sun* since it was computerized over forty years ago), and further demanded to see Bill Greener, whom he identified as his "editor."

The lone operator at the terminal at the time of the incident, Rupert Popkin, attempted to calm the intruder down, but as Popkin stated later, the man "went into a wild fit, repeating the names Woodward and Bernstein over and over and claiming he had been kidnapped by a UFO and put into suspended animation."

According to Popkin, who suffered minor cuts and bruises, the man then became violent and had to be taken into custody by security personnel, but somehow managed to escape while en route to Albany Complex Psychiatric Center. Witnesses at the scene reported that he ran off, shaking his fist at the sky and shouting, "I'll find you if it's the last thing I do!" As of this time, he remains at large.

Curiously, a check of files shows that an individual named Bill Greener did work at the *Sun* in the late twentieth century. However, no record of anyone named Nathan Halpern has been found.

SNNSLT GYRLHPT

by Michael Markiewicz

My father's saucer roared through the ionosphere leaving a streak of orange flame behind us. As we descended, the ship became coated with a thin glaze of frost and I could make out the ice sheet that capped the top of the Earth. We turned on the grav-well and shot across the North Pole like a giant, super-sonic, frozen wad of spit.

I knew we should enter the atmosphere over the poles so that we wouldn't be detected. But there's always the unlucky pilot who happens to come in at the wrong angle or at the wrong time of day.

Unfortunately, I happened to be that pilot today.

"They've got a lock on us from some place called 3DishNAR," said Krmak nervously, as a beeping alarm went off in the control panel.

Krmak was a smart kid, but he worried too much. This was a minor problem. We were now an unofficial blip on someone's radar screen.

"I'll shake them and they'll lose us in the grav-well's wake," I said.

"And just how will you do that? I think this is one of their new satellite arrays we were warned about in Advanced Flight."

Krmak liked to rub my nose in the fact that he had taken Advanced Flight this year.

"Just hold on," I said.

There was a moment of silence as I held the stick firmly to one side and rolled the craft in a spectacular spiral.

The saucer buzzed over the icy surface at nearly 13,000 miles per hour.

"I'm gonna . . . *uytorp!*"

"English, Krmak. English," I insisted, trying to read the gauges in the spinning cabin.

We had agreed to stick to either English or Spanish for the whole trip. If you're going to go to Earth you might as well learn some of the languages.

"Okay . . . in English . . . I'm gonna PUKE!"

And with that . . . he did.

It was a rancid puke. The sort you might have after eating too many raw clams. It smelled almost like a fermented bowl of beef stew—only without the bowl.

The problem was not the smell, however, or even the sight, of Krmak's lunch twirling around us like a wet whip of yellow-and-brown foam.

The problem was the moisture.

Krmak's spray plastered the controls and seeped into the tiny crevices between the dials and buttons. Instantly, I felt the ship yaw and shudder as one of the control rays shorted out.

"The balancing module is gone!" screamed Krmak.

"I know that!" I yelled, as the saucer rocked wildly. "Switch on the spare!"

Krmak threw open the control panel.

"I can't," he whined. "There's some other module in

here and I don't even know what it is! We're going to crash!"

"We're not going to crash!"

And we wouldn't, as long as nothing else went wrong.

I pulled the stick back and flipped through the manual overrides. The craft moaned. I pulled again. And then, finally, as the ice sheet nearly raked the bottom of our ship, we slowly gained altitude.

"You're nuts, Rillo," Krmak growled.

He might have taken Advanced Flight, but there was no substitute for sheer nerve and a little ignorance of normal physics.

I had just wiped myself off and was about to sit back and enjoy my triumph over the "puke fiasco," when Krmak gave me more "good" news.

"They've found us!" he cried, still wiping a string of spittle from his chin.

By now we had crossed over Hudson Bay and were heading into the airspace of the United States.

"They can't possibly catch us," I answered. "Let's just zip through on an arc course and let them eat our dust in the stratosphere."

"I don't know . . . " he argued.

At this point, my friend was really beginning to annoy me. He worried too much. And he puked too much.

"Krmak, I don't—"

"It's something new."

"I don't care—"

"They're approaching at mach five."

"Mach five?" I asked. "Earth doesn't have anything that fast."

"Mach six."

"Mach six?!"

"I've got an audible," Krmak said, switching on a speaker.

Our radio intercept crackled and hissed out the alien pilot's coded message. It took a few seconds for our computer to decrypt the signal, but it was simple enough.

"It's moving at nearly mach eighteen, but I think I can catch it," said the human.

"Aurora Six you are authorized to intercept and engage. I repeat: Engage," said the ground station.

Krmak looked at me oddly.

"Engage?" he asked.

I shrugged.

"I thought that meant when people get married."

It was two seconds later when we learned another meaning for "engage."

The missile smashed into us from the side at nearly twenty times the speed of sound. The explosion wrapped the entire outside of the ship in flame and sent us hurtling toward the ground.

"You were too low!" Krmak wailed.

But it was too late to argue.

As we streaked toward a remote area just south of a large lake, I quickly picked out a small field and prepared to land.

* * *

"How about, 'Gort, Klaatu Barrada Nicto'?" I suggested.

"I don't think so," replied my partner in crime.

"Why not? I think it sounds . . . cool. Cool, right?"

"That's not cool. Cool is something that's new and interesting, like *phlmmmghtttpp!* But what you said is from an ancient celluloid media tape—"

"You mean movies."

"—called *The Day the Earth Stood Still*. And we're not going to say anything! We have to get out of here without being detected. Do you want your father to get into trouble?"

Hmm. That was a good question. In a way . . . I did.

I was still mad about not getting my flying license. If I had to take his new saucer and break a few high council "non-contact" edicts to prove my point, so what? I was going to show my dad that I could pilot a saucer as well as anybody. When I came back with a log report that had actual interatmospheric penetration of an off-limits planet without being detected, he would have to let me get my license.

I guess my anger was obvious. Krmak looked at me and scowled. His longest tentacle reached out and tapped the control panel nervously.

"Gull juk tmmmmmm," he said smugly.

"We said we'd stick to English for the whole trip. Can't you speak it well enough to get your point across?"

I knew that would get him.

"Rillo," he said angrily, "I know you're mad at your dad, but this is serious. We can't get out of here without a balancing module!"

My nose twisted as I used it to scratch my middle eye.

"Don't scratch your eye at me!" Krmak snorted. "You're just lucky I decided to come along with you."

"You know, Krmak, sometimes you can really be a . . . a . . ."

"Loser? Killjoy? Stick in the mud?"

I glared. "Pick one. You're it."

"I came along with you because you're my friend and I don't want you to get killed."

Killed. Like some lame Earthlings could actually kill me.

"You came along because you wanted to see Earth for yourself. Admit it."

Krmak was a smart kid. He was always studying, especially about Earth. And I just knew that the way to get him to help me sneak my dad's saucer out for a little ride was to take him there.

He loved Earth ever since he was little and saw a transmission of *Sesame Street*. Once I told Krmak I was going to take my dad's saucer to the planet that made his favorite show, I knew he couldn't say no.

"Believe what you want, Rillo, but I wouldn't be so sure about not getting killed. Remember Tunguska?"

"Look," I assured him, "when they beamed his ship back up, they found out that it was Dogh's fault. He was just a bad pilot. The humans had nothing to do with his crash. And we're on the ground now so I don't think there's much chance of us burning up in a wreck."

"No, we're already a wreck!" he cried.

I liked Krmak, but one of these days I was going to find me a better best friend.

"We need to repair the balancing module, that's all," I said.

"Oh sure, like this technological wasteland is going to have them lying around in the woods! We're marooned, Rillo! We're dead! Do you hear me?! Dead! Expired! Deceased! *GYRLHPT!*"

"We're not *gyrlhpt,*" I insisted. "We're just—"

"Come on out of there with your hands up or I'll kill ya!" screeched a voice from outside the saucer.

Okay, we were *gyrlhpt.*

"Now what do we do?" Krmak snipped.

I looked at the screen to see just how bad it was. Were we surrounded by an entire army? Had the whole Earth been alerted and angry mobs assembled to wipe out the alien intruders? How bad could it be?

It was bad.

It was a girl.

It was a girl with red hair and blue eyes and soft pink lips that seemed to curl into a smile even when they were sneering and saying, "I'll blast a hole in you, if you don't come out right now!"

This was going to be trouble.

"Well?" said Krmak.

"Watch this," I said, taking the external microphone.

"Move back, Earthling!" I shouted. "Or we will be forced to use our, uh . . . laso-ray on you!"

"Laso-ray?" Krmak snickered.

We don't carry weapons. In fact, we outlawed all but defensive devices centuries ago.

"I never heard of a laso-ray," she replied. "You ever

heard of a Winchester? Well, it'll blast a hole right through this puny thing."

It was obvious this was not going to be easy. I'd never heard of a Winchester. I figured it was some sort of new lethal weapon the Earthlings used for wiping out alien visitors.

"If we stay here, maybe she can't shoot through the ship." Krmak thought aloud. "But if we stay here we'll never get a balancing module and eventually we'll starve to death."

"Thanks for the encouragement," I answered. "Look, what if we *do* go out there? She'd probably run screaming at the sight of us, right?"

"Why?"

"Humans are like that. They get scared of things they don't know. She sees us with our tentacles and three eyes and she'll probably take off for home so fast she'll drop that stupid gun. Then we can get out, find a module, and take off."

It was a plan—not a good one, but a plan.

I slowly opened the hatch and put the tip of a tentacle out just an inch.

"You better run, Earthling," I said in a hopeful rumble.

"Just come up out of there where I can see you!" shouted the female.

I decided I had had enough. I stood up and gave her my scariest *"BLHHHHAAAAAAZZT!"*

And when I looked down she was doing exactly what I expected. She was calmly pointing the weapon at my head.

"Now move on down here," she ordered.

"Is she scared?" asked Krmak beneath me.

"I don't think so," I replied.

In a few minutes she had both of us out of the ship and at barrel's end.

"Look," I began, "you don't really want to shoot us. We're friendly aliens. We even speak English."

"Don't mean nothing to me," she said with a sneer.

"I thought you said she'd be scared of us," Krmak mumbled.

The little alien crinkled her nose.

"I'm not scared of anything," she announced. "I saw you fly over our farm and crash in here and I got my gun so I could capture you. We're going to go back to my daddy's shop and I'm going to put you on TV and be famous."

This Earthling was loony. And a loony with a gun is never a good idea.

"TV?" Krmak smiled. "You can get us on TV? What about *Sesame Street*? Can we meet Big Bird? And Ernie?"

"KRMAK!" I shouted. "I don't think that's what she means."

"*Sesame Street*?" The vixen scowled. "That's kid's stuff."

"Well, we're kids, sort of," Krmak explained. "I'm about twelve in Earth years and Rillo here is about eleven. How old are you?"

She smiled and poked her chest.

"I'm nine, and don't forget it."

"Nine?" I asked.

"Earth years?" Krmak added.

That's when we took a good look at that gun. Come to think of it, most real guns don't have a big red plastic cap on the end with the words GENUINE ANNIE OAKLEY SURE SHOT written on the side.

"We're a couple of idiots," Krmak observed.

"Yeah. But we're a couple of *dead* idiots now." I pointed to the woods behind the little girl.

There was a small team of men running through the trees straight toward us. Most were wearing military-looking uniforms and carrying weapons—and these didn't say ANNIE OAKLEY SURE SHOT on the barrel.

"Nemesis Three to Red Fox, we have ground broken at Victor seven-niner, Alpha four!" shouted one into a communications device as he ducked behind a tree.

In an instant, a helicopter flew overhead and the men worked themselves into a line in front of us.

"Snnslt gyrlhpt," said Krmak.

Yes, we were *definitely* dead this time.

"Uh, look," I stammered. "We don't want any trouble. We were . . . just flying through. We don't mean any harm."

This sounded good, real convincing.

The men were standing about twenty yards off and several were pulling out what looked like guns with nets attached. They were probably going to net us, send us back to some lab for their evil experiments, and then put us on display in a zoo.

"Rssst yu ingruth bbme," said Krmak.

Like there was something we could do. *I* certainly couldn't think of anything. Our saucer was stuck. We were outnumbered, outgunned, and outmaneuvered.

At least until the little red menace spoke up.

"I know how we can get out of here," she whispered. "But you have to promise to be on my TV show."

Great—extortion from a nine-year-old.

"We'll do it," I answered.

The girl pointed down to a small ravine just behind our saucer.

"There's an old pipe down there that comes out at the base of our barn," she said softly. "We'll fit, but they won't, and they probably don't know where it goes."

"It's either that or we break every high council edict and wind up in some zoo," I figured.

Krmak nodded in agreement.

"Do not move!" said a voice from the crowd of men.

"What?" I said, standing in front of Krmak so he could jump first. He was definitely the slowest of the three of us.

"Oh good, you speak English. Don't move!" said the voice again, and this time I could see one of the net guns getting ready to fire.

"GO!" I shouted.

The girl ran ahead of Krmak and led the way down into the ditch.

Several pops went off overhead, and I saw one of the nets land just behind me. We scrambled through the vines and twisted undergrowth as the men chased after us.

"This way!" cried the redhead, pointing to a small metal pipe just big enough for us to crawl into. In a flash, she lunged inside the pipe and was gone.

"Come on!" she cried with an eerie echo.

The men had reached the top of the ravine.

"Engage!" shouted one.

Oh, we knew what *that* meant!

Krmak and I flew into that pipe so fast I thought I had left my skin back in the ravine.

"Go to the left here," said the girl as she crawled ahead.

We made the turn just in time to hear one of the net guns fire and see the snare miss my feet by inches.

"Come back here!" shouted one of the men. "Sergeant, get in there!"

Krmak and I shuffled behind the girl in the darkness as one of the soldiers struggled to follow us.

As we quickly put distance between us and the army we could hear a second man yelling, "I'm stuck! Get me out of here!"

"Okay, now come with me," insisted the girl.

We followed her out of the pipe, along the side of a barn and into a small shop. Over the door hung a sign: ED'S CHAIN SAW AND TV REPAIR.

"This doesn't look like a TV studio," whispered Krmak, as we stared at the hundreds of old and broken TV sets, radios, and assorted electronic junk.

Once inside, the girl smiled brightly and pointed at a tiny stage set with two chairs facing a home video camera on a tripod.

"This is where I tape my show," she announced. "I'm Deena and this is the Deena studio!"

"Deena studio?" asked Krmak.

"I'm using the back of my daddy's shop until I can

get an offer from one of the big stations to do my own show," she explained.

"We're a couple of idiots," I observed, yet again.

"Now you sit here and you come over here and I'll do the interview!"

"She must be kidding," Krmak whispered.

"You promised!" insisted Deena.

Krmak sat first. Deena made sure he was in the picture and asked me if I could run the camera.

"I can pilot a flying saucer, I think I can run a video camera," I replied sharply.

Actually, I didn't really understand a lot of the buttons, but I knew the basic idea.

"So," she began in her best "TV voice," "what planet are you from and what are you doing here on Earth?"

Krmak tried not to snicker.

"We're not really from a planet, it's more of an asteroid, and we're here because my friend, Rillo, over there was mad at his father for not letting him get his flying license. So we sort of took his saucer for an unscheduled ride."

"You stole it!"

"We didn't steal it," Krmak answered. "We just borrowed it . . . to prove that Rillo can fly."

"Hmm. I see," said the mini-reporter.

"But we were shot down by your Air Force and now our balancing module is broken."

"Can you tell the folks at home what a balancing module is?" she asked, pointing to the camera.

"I didn't have the heart to tell her there were no "folks at home."

"It's sort of like a tube with no air in it," Krmak explained. "It helps the ship maintain a level flight by adjusting the control rays. You can fly without it, but you can't take off or land."

"Is it dangerous?" she asked with wide eyes. "Could it wipe out the Earth?"

"No, nothing like that! It's just a piece of hardware. Like, like . . ."

And then it hit me.

"Like a television!" I shrieked.

"Huh?" said Krmak.

"Please wait for your interview," instructed Deena. "It doesn't look good to speak off-camera."

That's all we needed! One of the tubes from these old TVs could be plugged into the balancing module socket. It would probably burn out in a few minutes, but by that time we would be in space and wouldn't need it. Of course, we'd crash when we got home, but at least we'd get home.

"So, will you come and conquer the Earth someday?" she continued.

"Why?" asked Krmak blankly.

"Well, it's the most beautiful planet and you probably want our natural 'sources, right?"

Krmak chuckled.

"It's a nice place to visit, that's all," he replied.

After secretly taking the videotape out of the camera and hiding it in my pocket, I sat down and did my "interview." Deena definitely had a future as an investigative newshound.

I answered all her questions honestly, knowing that

none of it would ever get any farther than the wild imagination of a nine-year-old.

"Well, Deena," I added, after giving her a brief description of how antigravity drives work, "I'm afraid that if we don't get back to our world soon, we'll die."

"Die?" she asked suddenly.

"Die?!" yelped Krmak.

"Yes," I emphasized. "You see, Krmak and I can't breathe your air for more than a few hours before it kills us."

"It does?" she asked. "Oh, well . . ."

"IT DOES?!" wailed Krmak.

Like I said, Krmak was a smart kid, but not always.

"Yes, Krmak," I answered calmly. "Don't you remember that our teacher told us that *hyyt biun jyl tnn.*"

"Hey don't call me that!" said Krmak. "Oh . . . oh right, we *will* die if we don't get out of here right away."

"But what about your balancing thingy?" Deena asked.

"I think we could use one of these old TV tubes if your dad wouldn't mind," I said sheepishly.

"He won't mind," she agreed. "When he sees my video of a real live alien he won't care. Besides, most of these are broken, anyway."

"It doesn't matter, I added. "It will work as long as it's not cracked open."

We found a suitable "module" and got ready for our departure.

Of course, there was just one problem. Actually, it was about twenty or thirty problems all named sergeant or major or whatever and all standing around our saucer with guns to make sure we didn't get in it and fly off.

Deena agreed to help us sneak back to the area where we had crashed.

From the trees, we could see the men setting up a camp and temporary fencing around the crash site. They had posted guards throughout the woods and more men were arriving in trucks every few minutes.

"Snnslt gyrlhpt," said Krmak, surveying the almost impenetrable force.

"Well," I suggested, "maybe we could divert their attention."

"Like how?" said Krmak.

"I could run and make some noise," said Deena. "And then you could sneak into it when they're not looking."

It was a plan—just not a great one.

"Thank you, Deena," said Krmak. "For an alien, you're really pretty nice."

Deena smiled. "Will you come back someday and visit me?"

"If we get out of here alive," I answered, "and I still manage to get my flying license after all this, I promise we'll come back just to visit you."

And I meant it. Especially since I could not see any way we were going to get out of there.

"Bye," she said, gently shaking one of my tentacles.

Deena quickly ran to one side of the site and burst out from behind a bush.

"YAAAAAAA!" she screamed and dashed through the trees.

Krmak and I bolted for the saucer.

We were close. I could almost taste the freedom and see the clear blue sky disappearing beneath us.

Well, not that close.

We were about fifty yards away when we heard a crack and saw something fly through the air. Before we could take another step we felt the nets tangle us. In an instant, we were surrounded by the icy stares of the men.

We were on our way to a zoo for sure.

"Snnslt gyrlhpt," I said, noticing that Deena had also been netted.

"Yep," agreed Krmak. "We are deader than dead."

"They're probably going to dissect us or make us into circus freaks!" I grumbled.

"I don't know," said my friend.

"Or get us stuffed like some trophy!"

"Um, no I really don't think so—"

"I do!" I cried. "And I just want you to know that I'm . . . I'm sorry."

"No, Rillo, I mean that module in the control panel was—"

"Shut up and listen," I argued. "I know this is all my fault and I admit you were right. You were right about getting killed. You were right about us being marooned. And most of all, my dad was right about me not being ready to fly yet. If I were, then I wouldn't have gotten us in this mess in the first place."

There. At least I could die in peace.

"No," answered Krmak with a strange grin. "I meant it's going to be *worse* than being circus freaks or stuffed trophy heads."

"Worse?" I spit out, as our captors began shouting about something behind me. "How could it be worse? We're caught. Netted. And on our way to breaking every high council edict about Earth since it was discovered over two hundred years ago! What could *possibly* be worse?"

Through the tangled netting, Krmak pointed to the sky. He and the humans were looking at something.

"I think I know what was installed in place of the spare balancing module. I think your father put one of those new alarm systems with a homing beacon in his saucer."

As I twisted around in the net and looked up, I could see the trail of another saucer coming in fast. Its anti-grav tractor beam had already started to lift our wreckage. The men tried to shoot it down, but it was no use. As it hovered above us we could see the search ray scouting the area and we both knew it would only take a few minutes to find us.

In no time we would be aboard. The only evidence of our visit would be a top secret military report with no physical remains. Of course, Deena would probably entertain her parents for hours with her story of the three eyed, tentacled aliens, but they would chalk it up to her watching too many sci-fi TV shows. Someday I figured we would come back and see her to apologize, but in the meantime my father would take us home.

As the ray circled in around us we knew we were safe. We would be back in time for dinner . . . and we were *really* going to be *gyrlhpt*.

Mister Big

by Mark A. Garland

UFOs. Aliens. Creatures from outer space. Actually, I never believed in any of that stuff, until that night in late August, just a week before school started—which is where I suppose I should begin.

I was riding home on my bike near the woods on River Road, and they just grabbed me. It was about the only remarkable thing that had ever happened to me, at least up until that moment. I heard whirling noises, saw bright lights, smelled a whiff of something burning, and looked up just in time to see the ship stop, and hover overhead. Then it dropped some kind of purple beam of light on me, and my whole body started to tingle. Up I floated, bike and all, then the floor closed and I found myself in a smooth, rounded room that looked like the inside of a big eggshell.

I remember shaking, and asking, "Hey, what's happening?"

"Nothing good," said a strange and, well, alien voice, whiny and high-pitched.

"I'm sorry to hear that," I said, and I meant it.

"He's a very poor specimen," I heard another voice say.

"I'm sorry to hear that, too," I said. "I think."

"Weight to height ratio approximately double standard," the first whiner said. I guess I knew what that meant. A normal twelve-year-old kid my height usually weighs a little less than I do—well, okay, they usually weigh about *half* as much as I do, but it wasn't like I'd asked for any alien opinions.

They scanned me with a flashing, bright blue beam, spoke gibberish for a while, then turned me around and set me straight back down again on the road through the woods. I looked up and they were gone. By the time I got home I'd decided I must have imagined the whole thing—anyway, that's what I was telling myself. By the time I woke up the next morning I was fairly certain I'd dreamed the whole thing.

Maybe. Hopefully.

A few days later, the school year started, along with all the usual September events—new fall TV shows, the end of those awful hot days, and the advent of apple pie season—all of which helped me put the strange, alien experience behind me. That, and I'd discovered I had a new interest this year, something I'd suddenly begun to see in an entirely different way: girls. In fact, it didn't even take me till October to realize that the one thing I wanted more than anything else in the entire seventh grade was Lisa Cougan.

She was absolutely beautiful, from her long, dark-brown hair and big brown eyes to her junior cheerleader legs. I liked the way she walked, the way she smiled, the way she laughed. The only trouble was the way she looked at me when I said hello to her, like something didn't smell right and she'd just gotten a whiff of it. I couldn't blame her. She couldn't have weighed much more than 110 pounds, and without getting into too many details, well, you already know about me.

I sometimes thought that if I could just get to know her, talk to her a little, impress her with my wit and charm, that she might see me differently. That she might even, just once, really smile at me. I wanted to invite her to see a movie, or maybe have her over to my house so I could show her my comic book collection, or Playstation games, or my video collection, or all the trophies I'd won in pie eating contests—which was actually a proud family tradition; my parents made me look skinny by comparison.

But I knew she wouldn't come. It would have been easier to believe in UFOs. I'd never actually spoken to her at all, and I really couldn't even ask her. You have to know someone who knows someone in order to get to know someone in middle school, if you know what I mean. I didn't know anybody that knew Lisa Cougan, simple as that.

So I sat every day through the one regular class I shared with her, sitting too many seats away, imagining what she liked to talk about, what she was thinking about, what she'd be doing after school. I'd decided she had a personality a little like one of the girls in all those Disney movies: kind, sweet, smart, cute, wonderful!

I wished she would notice me, wished I'd lose sixty or seventy pounds, wished I was someone she knew . . . and liked.

Until that one fateful day when we crashed into each other.

She'd been headed up toward C Hall; I was headed for B Hall. We turned the corner at the same time and books, papers and Lisa went tumbling. I helped her up, gathered her things, said I was sorry.

"Yeah, me too," she said, sighing quite sweetly. Then she just stood there looking at me, and I thought I saw what might have been a smile starting to form on her perfect face. I felt my heart pounding, I couldn't breathe, I had to say something, anything—

"Would . . . would you go out with me?" I asked, though at the time I wasn't certain whether I'd actually said it out loud or just thought it in my head.

She made a lemon-juice face. "Go out with you?"

"Um, well . . . yes."

The sour look turned into a frown. "Only if you were the last boy on Earth," Lisa said. Then she walked off, down the hall, out of sight.

Living with the memory of that moment was bad enough, but on two days a week things got even worse.

There was nothing I dreaded more than Phys. Ed. class. Coach Judith always made us play games where we had to split up into two teams—coed teams. It didn't matter who were captains, I was always picked last, and the only reason I got picked at all was because someone had to choose me or we couldn't start the game. No one would pick me, although everyone would pick on me. "Billy is almost as round as the ball," they'd say, as we headed outside.

The girls would giggle, including Lisa, who seemed

especially amused. Then the jokes really started coming, kids yelling, "Stay out of Billy's way so you don't get crushed!" Or asking me to block the sun so they could see the ball. Or screaming at the top of their lungs, "Oh my God, we're gonna die!" if I was headed in their direction, then pretending they were in the middle of an earthquake when I ran by.

I wanted to crawl in a hole somewhere and just hide—I know, a really BIG hole.

But at the very beginning of the very last gym class I attended in the seventh grade, a couple of remarkable things happened, almost right in a row.

First, I got the ball for the first time that year.

Then I threw it, and it hit Lisa Cougan in the face.

She started howling and cursing, but no one blamed her. Her right eye was puffy and red, and tears were just streaming out of it. The coach told her to go inside and sit in the locker room for a while, and she'd be there in a minute to look at the eye. The game resumed, without me.

The coach had me sit on the sidelines and watch, just to be safe, I think. My team started winning almost right away. I sat there thinking this was probably the worst day of my entire life, which, all things considered, was quite a concept. I closed my eyes, trying not to cry.

And then the UFO appeared again.

The same one, I think—the same sounds, the same lights, same slight burning smell. Everyone looked up to see a gigantic silvery disk, nearly as big as the school, that seemed to have appeared out of nowhere. It hovered over the field, right above our heads. The sound grew louder, and a breeze arose that came from all directions at once and sent a chill straight through me, even though the breeze was warm.

The sound was attracting a lot of attention. Cars were stopping on the highway; kids started hanging out the school's windows, looking up. Suddenly, blinding bright beams of orange light flashed out of the UFO—moving lights that played across the roof of the school; flames burst wherever the beams touched it. In minutes, fire alarms wailing, the whole school was emptying out in all directions onto the playing fields that surrounded the building.

A moment later, lights flashed from the UFO again, though this time they were purple lights. I was pretty sure I knew what that meant.

Everyone started screaming right about then, even the coach. When the light touched me I felt a faint, familiar tingle, but nothing happened to me. The same was not true for everyone else. Like bubbles in a fresh glass of root beer, people started to disappear. Within seconds, the UFO had abducted just about everyone in my gym class.

Except me, of course. I hadn't been picked again!

That thought crushed something deep inside me, as I watched the UFO hover around the far side of the school, chasing panicked teachers and students wherever they ran, zapping them up into the spaceship. I had the feeling right then that the entire universe was basically sorry it had ever created me. I was so upset I wanted to cry.

Actually, I *did* start to cry. After all, there was practically no one left to see me. The UFO had taken almost all of them away.

"Why are you crying?" I heard a voice ask.

I turned and found Lisa standing there. I realized she'd come out of the building a little after the others, still holding one eye.

"Notice anything . . . um, different?" I asked, getting the sniffles under control.

Lisa frowned, one eyelid blinking at her surroundings. "Where is everybody?"

I thought about how I'd answer that, but there really wasn't any way to gloss things over.

"Okay, a giant UFO swooped down out of the sky and abducted them all," I said. "It's on the other side of the school right now, over the football field."

Lisa just stared at me for a moment, then she rolled her eyes and turned on her frown. "Very cute. Now, really, where are they? Where's the coach?"

"The aliens took her, too. No kidding."

Lisa glared at me then. "A giant UFO?"

"Yup."

Lisa stomped one foot on the grass. "Okay, I hate you!" she said. "I really hate you!"

Well, that wasn't quite news. "We probably ought to go tell somebody," I said.

"You just aren't going to quit, are you?"

"I'm telling the truth," I said.

"Right. Earth to Low Orbit, get a grip. And then—get away from me!"

"How's your eye?" I asked, trying to move things along. She seemed to be using it now.

"Better, no thanks to you."

I took a deep, frazzled breath. I was trying to rearrange a lot of things in my head about then. On the plus side we were having our longest conversation ever, but—

"You know, you're nothing like I expected," I said.

"What's that supposed to mean?" she snarled, still looking around.

"I thought you'd be—"

She turned back to me and I stopped. She looked ready to spit, and I couldn't think of one word that wouldn't get me wet.

"I'd be what?" she demanded.

I took another breath. "A little, you know, nicer."

"Huh! Why should I be nice to *you?*" she asked, the way you might ask your mother why you have to finish your vegetables. I didn't like vegetables very much, but the thought made my stomach growl. Then I heard a whooshing sound. I stared at my stomach in disbelief—until I realized the sound was coming from near the school. I looked up and saw the UFO moving back toward us, coming over the roof.

Lisa saw it, too.

"What's that?" she screamed—I mean really screamed—as the huge alien craft drew nearer. *"What is it? What is it?"*

I'd already told her, of course. Purple flashes leaped

from the UFO to the few remaining students scurrying past the edge of the school building onto the field. The UFO was almost on top of us. And then I did the only thing I could think of . . . which was to stand directly in front of Lisa.

"Stay behind me!" I told her. "And get down." She hesitated for an instant. "Please, just do it!"

She nodded, then did as I'd said. Now I was between her and the UFO. She didn't have any trouble hiding behind me; it was like hiding a softball behind a beach ball.

As the ship approached, its purple beam reached out and made me tingle again. Then the light passed by, and so did the UFO. I watched it snatch one or two missed kids, then the ship soared off, straight up into the sky.

"Okay," I said. "They're gone."

"That was fantastic!" Lisa said, so excited that she threw her arms around me. Tears ran down her face, and she was shaking. I put my arms around her, too.

"I'm still here!" she said. "What did you do? How did you do it?"

I looked at her. "They didn't see—" I stopped, and took another breath. "Well, they—um—they know better than to mess with me."

"I guess so!" Lisa said. She drew her head back and looked at me, still trying to catch her breath. "Anyway, you were right—we've got to tell somebody." She gave me another hug, then let go and started off the field at a trot.

"Hey!" I called after her, as I watched her head toward the empty school. I figured this was the best chance I'd ever get. "Do you think, maybe this weekend, if—if it's still there, I mean, we could go to the mall together . . . or . . . something?"

"Huh?" she said, stopping dead, glaring at me over her shoulder. I felt my heart pounding, I couldn't breathe. I wanted to say something, anything. But I'd said enough already.

"Didn't I tell you: only if you were last boy on Earth?" she said after a pause, though she was wearing a curious—possibly evil—grin.

I felt worse than ever. "Oh," I said softly.

Lisa folded her arms and surveyed the empty field. Then she wrinkled her nose at me, and smiled—a great big, genuine smile.

"Close enough," she said, holding out her hand. "Let's go!"

Like I said before, I never used to believe in weird stuff. But now I believe in a lot of things I used to wonder about—like creatures from outer space, and Lisa Cougan, and, of course . . . me.

DRAGON RESERVE, HOME EIGHT

by Diana Wynne Jones

Where to begin? Neal and I had had a joke for years about a little green van coming to carry me off—this was when I said anything more than usually mad—and now it was actually happening. Mother and I stood at my bedroom window watching the van bouncing up the track between the dun green hills, and neither of us smiled. It wasn't a farm van, and most of our neighbors visit on horseback anyway. Before long, we could see it was dark green with a silver dragon insigne on the side.

"It *is* the Dragonate," Mother said. "Siglin, there's nothing I can do." It astonished me to hear her say that. Mother only comes up to my shoulder, but she held her land and our household, servants, Neal and me, and all three of her husbands, in a hand like iron, *and* she drove out to plough or harvest if one of my fathers was ill. "They said the dragons would take you," she said. "I should have seen. You think Orm informed on you?"

"I know he did," I said. "It was my fault for going into the Reserve."

"I'll blood an axe on him," Mother said, "one of these days. But I can't do it over this. The neighbors would say he was quite right." The van was turning between the stone walls of the farmyard now. Chickens were squirting and flapping out of its way and our sheepdog pups were barking their heads off. I could see Neal up on the wash-house roof watching yearningly. It's a good place to watch from because you can hide behind the chimney. Mother saw Neal too. "Siglin," she said, "don't let on Neal knows about you."

"No," I said. "Nor you either."

"Say as little as you can, and wear the old blue dress—it makes you look younger," Mother said, turning towards the door. "You might just get off. Or they might just have come about something else," she added. The van was stopping outside the front door now, right underneath my window. "I'd best go and greet them," Mother said, and hurried downstairs.

While I was forcing my head through the blue dress, I heard heavy boots on the steps and a crashing knock at the door. I shoved my arms into the sleeves, in too much of a hurry even to feel indignant about the dress. It makes me look about twelve and I am nearly grown up! At least, I was fourteen quite a few weeks ago now. But Mother was right. If I looked too immature to have awakened, they might not question me too hard. I hurried to the head of the stairs while I tied my hair with a childish blue ribbon. I knew they had come for me, but I had to *see.*

They were already inside when I got there, a whole line of tall men tramping down the stone hallway in the half-dark, and Mother was standing by the closed front door as if they had swept her aside. What a lot of them, just for me! I thought. I got a weak, sour feeling and could hardly move for horror. The man at the front of the line kept opening the doors all down the hallway, calm as you please, until he came to the main parlor at the end. "This room will do nicely," he said. "Out you get, you." And my oldest father, Timas, came shuffling hurriedly out in his slippers, clutching a pile of accounts and looking scared and worried. I saw Mother fold her arms. She always does when she is angry.

Another of them turned to Mother. "We'll speak to you first," he said, "and your daughter after that. Then we want the rest of the household. Don't any of you try to leave." And they went into the parlor with Mother and shut the door.

They hadn't even bothered to guard the doors. They just assumed we would obey them. I was shaking as I walked back to my room, but it was not terror any more. It was rage. I mean—we have all been brought up to honor the Dragonate. They are the cream of the men of the Ten Worlds. They are supposed to be gallant and kind and dedicated and devote their lives to keeping us safe from Thrallers, not to speak of maintaining justice, law and order all over the Ten Worlds. Dragonate men swear that Oath of Alienation, which means they can never have homes or families like ordinary people. Up to then, I'd felt sorry for them for that. They give up so much. But now I saw they felt it gave them the right to behave as if the rest of us were not real people. To walk in as if they owned our house. To order Timas out of his own parlor. Oh I was angry!

I don't know how long Mother was in the parlor. I was so angry it felt like seconds until I heard flying feet and Neal hurried into my room. "They want you now."

I stood up and took some of my anger out on poor Neal. I said, "Do you still want to join the Dragonate? Swear that stupid Oath? Behave like you own the Ten Worlds?"

It was mean. Neal looked at the floor. "They said straight away," he said. Of course he wanted to join. Every boy does, particularly on Sveridge, where women own most of the land. I swept down the stairs, angrier than ever. All the doors in the hallway were open and our people were standing in them, staring. The two housemen were at the dining-room door, the cattlewoman and two farmhands were looking out of the kitchen, and the stableboy and the second shepherd were craning out of the pantry. I thought, They still will be my people some day! I refuse to be frightened! My fathers were in the doorway of the bookroom. Donal and Yan were in work-clothes and had obviously rushed in without taking their boots off. I gave them what I hoped was a smile, but only Timas smiled back. They all know! I thought as I opened the parlor door.

There were only five of them, sitting facing me across our best table. Five was enough. All of them stood up as I came in. The room seemed full of towering green uniforms. It was not at all like I expected. For one thing, the media always shows Dragonate as fair and dashing and handsome, and none of these were. For another, the media had led me to expect uniforms with big silver panels. These were all plain green, and four of them had little silver stripes on one shoulder.

"Are you Sigrid's daughter Siglin?" asked the one who had opened all the doors. He was a bleached, pious type like my father Donal and his hair was dust-color.

"Yes," I said rudely. "Who are you? Those aren't Dragonate uniforms."

"Camerati, lady," said one who was brown all over with wriggly hair. He was young, younger than my father Yan, and he smiled cheerfully, like Yan does. But he made my stomach go cold. Camerati are the crack force, cream of the Dragonate. They say a man has to be a genius even to be considered for it.

"Then what are you doing here?" I said. "And why are you all standing up?"

The one in the middle, obviously the chief one, said, "We always stand up when a lady enters the room. And we are here because we were on a tour of inspection at Holmstad anyway, and there was a Slaver scare on this morning. So we offered to take on civic duties for the regular Dragonate. Now if that answers your questions, let me introduce us all." He smiled too, which twisted his white, crumpled face like a demon mask. "I am Lewin, and I'm Updriten here. On your far left is Driten Palino, our recorder." This was the pious type, who nodded. "Next to him is Driten Renick of Law Wing." Renick was elderly and iron-grey, with one of those necks that looks like a chicken's leg. He just stared. "Underdriten Terens is on my left, my aide and witness." That was brown-and-wriggly. "And beyond him is Cadet Alectis, who is traveling with us to Home Nine."

Alectis looked a complete baby, only a year older than me, with pink cheeks and sandy hair. He and Terens both bowed and smiled so politely that I nearly smiled back. Then I realized that they were treating me as if I was a visitor. In my own home! I bowed freezingly, the way Mother usually does to Orm.

"Please sit down, Siglin," Lewin said politely.

I nearly didn't, because that might keep them standing up too. But they were all so tall I'd already got a crick in my neck. So I sat grandly on the chair they'd put facing the table. "Thank you," I said. "You are a very kind host, Updriten Lewin." To my great joy, Alectis went bright red at that, but the other four simply sat down too. Pious Palino took up a memo block and poised his fingers over its keys. This seemed to be in case the recorder in front of Lewin went wrong. Lewin set that going. Wriggly Terens leaned over and passed me another little square box.

"Keep this in your hand," he said, "or your answers may not come out clearly."

I caught the words *lie detector* from his wriggly head as clearly as if he had said them aloud. I don't think I showed how very scared I was, but my hand made the box wet almost straight away.

"Court is open," Lewin said to the recorder. "Presiding Updriten Lewin." He gave a string of numbers and then said, "First hearing starts on charges against Siglin, of Upland Holding, Wormstow, North Sveridge on Home Eight, accused of being heg and heg concealing its nature. Questions begin. Siglin, are you clear what being heg is?" He crumpled one eyebrow upwards at me.

"No," I said. After all, no one has told me in so many words. It's just a thing people whisper and shudder at.

"Then you'd better understand this," Lewin said. He really was the ugliest and most outlandish of the five. Dragonate men are never posted to the world of their birth, and I thought Lewin must come from one a long way off.

His hair was black, so black it had blue lights, but, instead of being dark all over to match it, like wriggly Terens, he was a lot whiter than me and his eyes were a most piercing blue—almost the color they make the sky on the media. "If the charges are proved," he said, "you face death by beheading, since that is the only form of execution a heg cannot survive. Renick—"

Elderly Renick swept sourly in before Lewin had finished speaking. "The law defines a heg as one with human form who is not human. Medical evidence of brain pattern or nerve and muscle deviations is required prior to execution, but for a first hearing it is enough to establish that the subject can perform one or more of the following: mind-reading, kindling fire or moving objects at a distance, healing or killing by the use of the mind alone, surviving shooting, drowning or suffocation, or enslaving or otherwise afflicting the mind of a beast or human."

He had the kind of voice that bores you anyway. I thought, Great gods! I don't think I can do half those things! Maybe I looked blank. Palino stopped clicking his memo block to say, "It's important to understand why these creatures must be stamped out. They can make people into puppets in just the same way that the Slavers can. Foul." Actually, I think he was explaining it to Alectis. Alectis nodded humbly. Palino said, definitely to me, "Slavers can do it with those V-shaped collars. You must have seen them on the media. Quite foul."

"We call them Thrallers," I said. Foul or not, I thought, I'm the only one of me I've got! I can't help being made the way I am.

Lewin flapped his hand to shut Palino up and Renick went on again. "A heg is required by law to give itself up for execution. Any normal person who knowingly conceals a heg is likewise liable for execution." Now I knew why Mother had told me to keep Neal out of it.

Then it seemed to be Palino's turn. He said, "Personal details follow. How old are you—er—Sigrun?"

"Sig*lin,*" I said. "Fourteen last month."

Renick stretched out his chicken neck. "In this court's opinion, subject is old enough to have awakened as heg." He looked at Terens.

Terens said, "I witness. Girls awaken early, don't they?"

Palino, tapping away, said, "Mother, Sigrid, also of Upland Holding."

At which Lewin leaned forward. "Cleared by this court," he said. I was relieved to hear that. Mother is clever. She hadn't let them know she knew.

Palino said, "And your father is—?"

"Timas, Donal and Yan," I said. I had to bite the inside of my cheek not to laugh at how annoyed he was by that.

"Great Tew, girl!" he said. "A person can't have three fathers!"

"Hold it, Palino," said Lewin. "You're up against local customs here. Men outnumber women three to one on Home Eight."

"In Home Eight law, a woman's child is the child of all her husbands equally," Renick put in. "No more anomalous than the status of the Ahrings on Seven really."

"Then tell me how I rephrase my question," Palino said

waspishly, "in the light of the primitive customs of Home Eight."

I said, "There's no such place as Home Eight. This world is called Sveridge." Primitive indeed!

Palino gave me a pale glare. I gave him one back. Lewin cut in, smooth and humorous, "You're up against primitive Dragonate custom here, Siglin. We refer to all worlds by numbers, from Albion, Home One, to Yurov, Home Ten, and the worlds of the Outer Manifold are Cath One, Two, Three and Four to us. Have you really no idea which of your mother's husbands is actually your father?"

After that they all began asking me. Being heg is inherited, and I knew they were trying to find out if any of my fathers was heg too. At length even Alectis joined in, clearing his throat and going very red because he was only a Cadet. "I know we're not supposed to know," he said, "but I bet you've tried to guess. I did. I found out in the end."

That told me he was Sveridge too. And he suddenly wasn't a genius in the Camerati any more, but just a boy. "Then I bet you wished you hadn't!" I said. "My friend Inga at Hillfoot found out, and hers turned out to be the one she's always hated."

"Well," said Alectis, redder still. "Er—it wasn't the one I'd hoped—"

"That's why I've never asked," I said. And that was true. I'd always hoped it was Timas till now. Donal is so moral, and Yan is fun, but he's under Donal's thumb even more than he's under Mother's. But I didn't want my dear old Timas in trouble.

"Well, a cell-test should settle it," Lewin said. "Memo

for that, Palino. Terens, remind me to ask how the regular Dragonate usually deal with it. Now—Siglin, this charge was laid against you by a man known as Orm the Worm Warden. Do you know this man?"

"Don't I just!" I said. "He's been coming here and looking through our windows and giggling ever since I can remember! He lives on the Worm Reserve in a shack. Mother says he's a bit wrong in the head, but no one's locked him up because he's so good at managing dragons."

There! I thought. That'll show them you can't trust a word Orm says! But they just nodded. Terens murmured to Alectis, "Sveridge worm, *Draco draco*, was adopted as the symbol of the Dragonate—"

"We *have* all heard of dragons," Palino said to him nastily.

Lewin cut in again. I suppose it was his job as presiding Updriten. "Siglin. Orm, in his deposition, refers to an incident in the Worm Reserve last Friday. We want you to tell us what happened then, if anything."

Grim's teeth! I thought. I'd hoped they'd just ask me questions. You can nearly always get around questions without lying. And I'd no idea what Orm had said. "I don't usually go to the Dragon Reserve," I said, "because of being Mother's heir. When I was born, the Fortune Teller said the dragons would take me." I saw Renick and Palino exchange looks of contempt at our primitive customs. But Mother had in a good Teller, and I believe it enough to keep away from the Reserve.

"So why did you go last Friday?" said Lewin.

"Neal dared me to," I said. I couldn't say anything else

with a lie detector in my hands. Neal gets on with Orm, and he goes to the Reserve a lot. Up to Friday, he thought I was being silly refusing to go. But the real trouble was that Neal had been there all along, riding Barra beside me on Nellie, and now Lewin had made me mention Neal, I couldn't think how to pretend he hadn't been there. "I rode up behind Wormhill," I said, "and then over the Saddle until we could see the sea. That means you're in the Reserve."

"Isn't the Reserve fenced off at all?" Renick asked disapprovingly.

"No," I said. "Worms—dragons—can fly, so what's the point? They stay in because the shepherds bombard them if they don't, and we all give them so many sheep every month." And Orm makes them stay, bad cess to him! "Anyway," I said, "I was riding down a kyle—that's what we call those narrow stony valleys—when my horse reared and threw me. Next thing I knew—"

"Question," said Palino. "Where was your brother at this point?"

He *would* spot that! I thought. "Some way behind," I said. Six feet, in fact. Barra is used to dragons and just stood stock-still. "This dragon shuffled head down with its great snout across the kyle," I said. "I sat on the ground with its great amused eye staring at me and listened to Nellie clattering away up the kyle. It was a youngish one, sort of brown-green, which is why I hadn't seen it. They can keep awfully still when they want to. And I said a rude word to it.

"'That's no way to speak to a dragon!' Orm said. He

was sitting on a rock on the other side of the kyle, quite close, laughing at me." I wondered whether to fill the gap in the story where Neal was by telling them that Orm always used to be my idea of Jack Frost when I was little. He used to call at Uplands for milk then, to feed dragon fledglings on, but he was so rude to Mother that he goes to Inga's place now. Orm is long and skinny and brown, with a great white bush of hair and beard, and he smells rather. But they must have smelt him in Holmstad, so I said, "I was scared, because the dragon was so near I could feel the heat off it. And then Orm said, 'You have to speak politely to this dragon. He's my particular friend. You give me a nice kiss, and he'll let you go.' "

I think Lewin murmured something like, "Ah, I thought it might be that!" but it may just have been in his mind. I don't know because I was in real trouble then, trying to pick my way through without mentioning Neal. The little box got so wet it nearly slipped out of my hand. I said, "Every time I tried to get up, Orm beckoned, and the dragon pushed me down with its snout with a gamesome look in its eye. And Orm cackled with laughter. They were both really having fun." This was true, but the dragon also pushed between me and Neal and mantled its wings when Neal tried to help. And Neal said some pretty awful things to Orm. Orm giggled and insulted Neal back. He called Neal a booby who couldn't stand up for himself against women. "Then," I said, "then Orm said I was the image of Mother at the same age—which isn't true; I'm bigger all over—and he said, 'Come on, kiss and be friends!' Then he skipped down from his rock and took hold of my arm—"

I had to stop and swallow there. The really awful thing was that, as soon as Orm had hold of me, I got a strong picture from his mind: Orm kissing a pretty lady smaller than me, with another dragon, an older, blacker one, looking on from the background. And I recognized the lady as Mother, and I was absolutely disgusted.

"So I hit Orm and got up and ran away," I said. "And Orm shouted at me all the time I was running up the kyle and catching Nellie, but I took no notice."

"Question," said Renick. "What action did the dragon take?"

"They—they always chase you if you run, I'd heard," Alectis said shyly.

"And this one appears to have been trained to Orm's command," Palino said.

"It didn't chase me," I said. "It stayed with Orm." The reason was that neither of them could move. I still don't know what I did—I had a picture of myself leaning back inside my own head and swinging mighty blows, the way you do with a pickaxe—and Neal says the dragon went over like a cartload of potatoes and Orm fell flat on his back. But Orm could speak and he screamed after us that I'd killed the worm and I'd pay for it. But I was screaming too, at Neal, to keep away from me because I was heg. That was the thing that horrified me most. Before that I'd tried not to think I was. After all, for all I knew, everyone can read minds and get a book from the bookcase without getting up from their chair. And Neal told me to pull myself together and think what we were going to tell Mother. We decided to say that we'd met a dragon in the Reserve and

I'd killed it and found out I was heg. I made Neal promise not to mention Orm. I couldn't bear even to think of Orm. And Mother was wonderfully understanding, and I really didn't realize that I'd put her in danger as well as Neal.

Lewin looked down at the recorder. "Dragons are a preserved species," he said. "Orm claims that you caused grievous bodily harm to a dragon in his care. What have you to say to that?"

"How could I?" I said. Oh I was scared. "It was nearly as big as this house."

Renick was on to that at once. "Query," he said. "Prevarication?"

"Obviously," said Palino, clicking away at his block.

"We haven't looked at that dragon yet," Terens said.

"We'll do that on our way back," Lewin said, sighing rather. "Siglin, I regret to say there is enough mismatch between your account and Orm's, and enough odd activity on that brain-measure you hold in your hand, to warrant my taking you to Holmstad Command Center for further examination. Be good enough to go with Terens and Alectis to the van and wait there while we complete our inquiries here."

I stood up. Everything seemed to drain out of me. I could lam them like I lammed that dragon, I thought. But Holmstad would only send a troop out to see why they hadn't come back. And I put my oldest dress on for nothing! I thought as I walked down the hallway with Terens and Alectis. The doors were all closed. Everyone had guessed. The van smelt of clean plastic and it was very warm and light because the roof was one big window. I sat between Terens and Alectis on the back seat. They pulled straps round us all—safety straps, but they made me feel a true prisoner.

After a while, Terens said, "You could sue Orm if the evidence doesn't hold up, you know." I think he was trying to be kind, but I couldn't answer.

After another while, Alectis said, "With respect, Driten, I think suspects should be told the truth about the so-called lie detector."

"Alectis, I didn't hear you say that," Terens said. He pretended to look out of the window, but he must have known I knew he had deliberately thought *lie detector* to me as he passed me the thing. They're told to. Dragonate think of everything. I sat and thought I'd never hated anything so much as I hated our kind, self-sacrificing Dragonate, and I tried to take a last look at the stony yard, tipped sideways on the hill, with our square stone house at the top of it. But it wouldn't register somehow.

Then the front door opened and the other three came out, bringing Neal with them. Behind them, the hall was full of our people, with Mother in front, just staring. I just stared too, while Palino opened the van door and shoved Neal into the seat beside me. "Your brother has admitted being present at the incident," he said as he strapped himself in beside Neal. I could tell he was pleased.

By this time, Lewin and Renick had strapped themselves into the front seat. Lewin drove away without a word. Neal looked back at the house. I couldn't. "Neal—?" I whispered.

"Just like you said," Neal said, loudly and defiantly.

"Behaving as if they own the Ten Worlds. I wouldn't join now if they begged me to!" Why did I have to go and say that to him? "Why did *you* join?" Neal said rudely to Alectis.

"Six brothers," Alectis said, staring ahead.

The other four all started talking at once. Lewin asked Renick the quickest way to the Reserve by road and Renick said it was down through Wormstow. "I hope the dragons eat you!" Neal said. This was while Palino was leaning across us to say to Terens, "Where's our next inspection after this hole?" And Terens said, "We go straight on to Arkloren on Nine. Alectis will get to see some other parts of the Manifold shortly." Behaving as if we didn't exist. Neal shrugged and shut up.

The Dragonate van was much smoother and faster than a farm van. We barely bounced over the stony track that loops down to Hillfoot, and it seemed no time before we were speeding down the better road, with the rounded yellowish Upland Hills peeling past on either side. I love my hills, covered with yellow ling that only grows here on Sveridge, and the soft light of the sun through our white and grey clouds. Renick, still making conversation, said he was surprised to find the hills so old and worn down. "I thought Eight was a close parallel with Seven!" he said.

Lewin answered in a boring voice, "I wouldn't know. I haven't seen Seven since I was a Cadet."

"Oh, the mountains are much higher and greener there," Renick said. "I was posted in Camberia for years. Lovely spot."

Lewin just grunted. Quite a wave of homesickness filled

the van. I could feel Renick thinking of Seven and Alectis not wanting to go to Nine. Terens was remembering boating on Romaine when he was Neal's age. Lewin was thinking of Seven, in spite of the grunt. We were coming over Jiot Fell already then, with the Giant Stones standing on top of the world against the sky. A few more turns in the road would bring us out above Wormstow where Neal and I went—used to go—to school. What about me? I was thinking. I'm homesick for life. And Neal. Poor Mother.

Then the air suddenly filled with noise, like the most gigantic sheet being torn.

Lewin said, "What the—?" and we all stared upwards. A great silvery shape screamed overhead. And another of a fatter shape, more blue than silver, screamed over after it, both of them only just inside the clouds. Alectis put up an astonished pointing arm. "Thraller! The one behind's a Slaver!"

"What's it doing *here?*" said Terens. "Someone must have slipped up."

"Ours was a stratoship!" said Palino. "What's going on?"

A huge ball of fire rolled into being on the horizon, above the Giant Stones. I felt Lewin slam on the brakes. "We got him!" one of them cried out.

"The Slaver got ours," Lewin said. The brakes were still yelling like a she-worm when the blast hit.

I lose the next bit. I start remembering again a few seconds later, sitting up straight with a bruised lip, finding the van round sideways a long way on down the road. In front of me, Renick's straps had broken. He was lying kind of folded against the windscreen. I saw Lewin pull himself upright and pull at Renick. And stop pulling quickly. My ears had gone deaf, because I could only hear Lewin as if he was very far off. "—hurt in the back?"

Palino looked along the four of us and shouted, "Fine! Is Renick—?"

"Dead," Lewin shouted back. "Neck broken." He was jiggling furiously at buttons in the controls. My ears started to work again and I heard him say, "Holmstad's not answering. Nor's Ranefell. I'm going back to Holmstad. Fast."

We set off again with a roar. The van seemed to have lost its silencer and it rattled all over, but it went. And how it went. We must have done nearly a hundred down Jiot, squealing on the bends. In barely minutes, we could see Wormstow spread out below, old grey houses and new white ones, and all those imported trees that make the town so pretty. The clouds over the houses seemed to darken and go dense.

"Uh-oh!" said Terens.

The van jolted to another yelling stop. It was not the clouds. Something big and dark was coming down through the clouds, slowly descending over Wormstow. Something enormous. "What *is* that?" Neal and Alectis said together.

"Hedgehog," said Terens.

"A slaveship," Palino explained, sort of mincing the word out to make it mean more. "Are—are we out of range here?"

"I most thoroughly hope so," Lewin said. "There's not much we can do with hand weapons."

We sat and stared as the thing came down. The lower it got, the more Renick's bent-up shape was in my way. I kept wishing Lewin would do something about him, but nobody seemed to be able to think of anything but that huge descending ship. I saw why they call them hedgehogs. It was rounded above and flat beneath, with bits and pieces sticking out all over like bristles. Hideous somehow. And it came and hung squatting over the roofs of the houses below. There it let out a ramp like a long black tongue, right down into the Market Square. Then another into High Street, between the rows of trees, breaking a tree as it passed.

As soon as the ramps touched ground, Lewin started the van and drove down towards Wormstow.

"No, stop!" I said, even though I knew he couldn't. The compulsion those Slavers put out is really strong. Some of it shouts inside your head, like your own conscience through an amplifier, and some of it is gentle and creeping and insidious, like Mother telling you gently to come along now and be sensible. I found I was thinking, Oh well, I'm sure Lewin's right. Tears rolled down Alectis's face, and Neal was sniffing. We had to go to the ship, which was now hanging a little above us. I could see people hurrying out of houses and racing to crowd up the ramp in the Market Square. People I knew. So it must be all right, I thought. The van was having to weave past loose horses that people had been riding or driving. That was how I got a glimpse of the other ramp, through trees and the legs of a horse. Soldiers were pouring down it, running like a muddy river, in waves. Each wave had a little group of kings, walking behind it, directing the soldiers. They had shining crowns and shining Vs on their chests and walked mighty, like gods.

That brought me to my senses. "Lewin," I said. "Those are Thrallers and you're *not* to do what they say, do you hear?" Lewin just drove round a driverless cart, towards the Market Square. He was going to be driving up that ramp in a second. I was so frightened then that I lammed Lewin—not like I lammed the dragon, but in a different way. Again it's hard to describe, except that this time I was giving orders. Lewin was to obey *me,* not the Thrallers, and my orders were to drive away *at once.* When nothing seemed to happen, I got so scared that I seemed to be filling the whole van with my orders.

"Thank you," Lewin said, in a croaking sort of voice. He jerked the van round into Worm Parade and roared down it, away from the ship and the terrible ramps. The swerve sent the van door open with a slam and, to my relief, the body of poor Renick tumbled out into the road.

But everyone else screamed out, "No! What are you doing?" and clutched their heads. The compulsion was far, far worse if you disobeyed. I felt as if layers of my brain were being peeled off with hot pincers. Neal was crying, like Alectis. Terens was moaning. It hurt so much that I filled the van frantically with more and more orders. Lewin made grinding sounds, deep in his throat, and kept on driving away, with the door flapping and banging.

Palino took his straps undone and yelled, "You're going the wrong way, you damn cariarder!" I couldn't stop him at all. He started to climb into the front seat to take the controls away from Lewin. Alectis and Neal both rose up too and shoved him off Lewin. So Palino gave that up and scrambled for the open flapping door instead. Nobody could do a thing. He just jumped out and went rolling in the road. I didn't see what he did then, because I was too busy giving orders, but Neal says he simply scrambled up and staggered back towards the ship and the ramp.

We drove for another horrible half-mile, and then we must have got out of range. Everything suddenly went easy. It was like when somebody lets go the other end of a rope you're both pulling, and you go over backwards. Wham. And I felt too dim and stunned to move.

"Thank the gods!" I heard Terens more or less howl.

"It's Siglin you should be thanking," Lewin said. "Alectis, climb over to the front and shut that door. Then try and raise Holmstad again."

Neal says the door was too battered to shut. Alectis had to hold it with one hand while he worked the broadcaster with the other. I heard him saying that Holmstad still didn't answer through the roaring and rattling the van made when Lewin put on speed up the long looping gradient of Wormjiot. We hadn't nearly got up to the Saddle, when Terens said, "It's going! Aren't they quick!" I looked back, still feeling dim and horrible, in time to see the squatting hedgehog rise up inside the clouds again.

"Now you can thank the gods," Lewin said. "They didn't think we were worth chasing. Try medium wave, Alectis." There is an outcrop of ragged rock near the head of Wormjiot. Lewin drove off the road and stopped behind it while Alectis fiddled with knobs.

Instead of getting dance music and cookery hints, Alectis got a voice that fizzled and crackled. "This is Dragonate Fanejiot, Sveridge South, with an emergency message for all Dragonate units still in action. You are required to make your way to Fanejiot and report there soonest." It said that about seven times, then it said, "We can now confirm earlier reports that Home Nine is in Slaver hands. Here is a list of bases on Home Eight that have been taken by Slavers." It was a long list. Holmstad came quite early on it, and Ranefell about ten names after that.

Lewin reached across and turned it off. "Did someone say we slipped up?" he said. "That was an understatement."

"Fanejiot is two thousand flaming miles from here!" Terens said. "With an ocean and who knows how many Slavers in between!"

"Well put," said Lewin. "Did Palino's memo block go to the Slavers with him?"

It was lying on the back seat beside Neal. Neal tried to pretend it wasn't, but Alectis turned round and grabbed it as Neal tried to shove it on the floor. I was lying back in my straps, feeling grey and thinking, We could get away now. I'd better lam them all again. But all I did was lie there and watch Neal and Alectis having an angry tug-of-war. Then watch Lewin turn round and pluck the block from the pair of them.

"Don't be a fool," he said to Neal. "I've already erased the recorder. And if I hadn't had Renick and Palino breathing righteously down our necks, I'd never have recorded anything. It goes against the grain to take in children."

Lewin pressed the *erase* on the memo block and it gave

out a satisfied sort of gobble. Neither of the other two said anything, but I could feel Alectis thinking how much he had always hated Palino. Terens was looking down at Wormstow through a fieldglass and trying not to remember a boy in Cadets with him who had turned heg and given himself up. I felt I wanted to say thank you. But I was too shy to do anything but sit up and look at Wormstow too, between the jags of the rock. Even without a fieldglass, I could see the place throbbing like a broken anthill with all the Slaver troops.

"Getting ready to move out and mop up the countryside," Terens said.

"Yes, and that's where most people live," Lewin said. "Farms and holdings in the hills. What's the quickest way to the Dragon Reserve?"

"There's a track on the right round the next bend," said Neal. "Why?"

"Because it's the safest place I can think of," Lewin said.

Neal and I looked at one another. You didn't need to be heg to tell that Neal was thinking, just as I was, that this was a bit much. They were supposed to help all those people in the holdings. Instead, they thought of the safest place and ran there! So neither of us said that the track was only a bridle path, and we didn't try to warn them not to take the van into the Reserve. We just sat there while Lewin drove it uphill, and then lumping and bumping and rattling up the path. The path gave out in the marshy place below the Saddle, but Lewin kept grinding and roaring on, throwing up peat in squirts, until we tipped downhill again and bounced down a yellow fellside. We were in the Reserve by then. The ling was growing in lurid green patches, black at the roots, where dragons had burnt it in the mating season. They fight a lot then.

We got some way into the Reserve. The van gave out clanging sounds and smelt bad, but Lewin kept it going by driving on the most level parts. We were in a wide stony scoop, with yellow hills all round, when the smell got worse and the van just stopped. Alectis let go of the door. "Worms—dragons," he said, "don't like machines, I've heard."

"Now he tells us!" said Terens, and we all got out. We all looked as if we had been in an accident—I mean, I know we had in a way, but we looked worse than I'd expected: sort of ragged and pale and shivery. Lewin turned his foot on a stone, which made him clutch his chest and swear. Neither of the other two even asked if he was all right. That is the Dragonate way. They just set out walking. Neal and I went with them, thinking of the best place to dodge up a kyle, so that we could run home and try and warn Mother about the Slavers.

"Where that bog turns into a stream—I'll say when," Neal was whispering, when a dragon came over the hill into the valley and made straight for us.

"Stand still!" said Alectis. Lewin and Terens each had a gun in their hand without seeming to have moved. Alectis didn't, and he was white.

"They only eat moving prey," Neal said, because he was sorry for him. "Make sure not to panic and run and you're fine."

I was sorry for Alectis too, so I added, "It's probably only after the van. They love metal."

Lewin crumpled his face at me and said "Ah!" for some reason.

The dragon came quite slowly, helping itself with its spread wings and hanging its head rather. It was a bad color, sort of creamy through the brown-green. I thought it might be one of the sick ones that turn man-eater, and I tried to brace myself and stop feeling so tired and shaky so that I could lam it. But Neal said, "That's Orm's dragon! You didn't kill it after all!"

It *was* Orm's dragon. By this time, it was near enough for me to see the heat off it quivering the air, and I recognized the gamesome, shrewd look in its eye. But since it had every reason to hate me, that didn't make me feel much better. It came straight for me too. We all stood like statues. And it came right up to me and bent its neck, and laid its huge brown head on the ling in front of my feet, where it puffed out a sigh that made Lewin cough and gasp another swearword. It had felt me coming, the dragon said, and it was here to say sorry. It hadn't meant to upset me. It had thought it was a game.

That made me feel terrible. "I'm sorry too," I said. "I lost my head. I didn't meant to hurt you. That was Orm's fault."

Orm was only playing too, the dragon said. Orm called him Huffle, and I could too if I liked. Was he forgiven? He was ashamed.

"Of course I forgive you, Huffle," I said. "Do you forgive me?"

Yes. Huffle lifted his head up and went a proper color at once. Dragons are like people that way.

"Ask him to fetch Orm here," Lewin said urgently.

I didn't want to see Orm, and Lewin was a coward. "Ask him yourself," I said. "He understands."

"Yes, but I don't think he'd do it for me," Lewin said.

"Then, will you fetch Orm for Lewin?" I asked Huffle.

He gave me a cheeky look. Maybe. Presently. He sauntered away past Terens, who moved his head back from Huffle's rattling right wing, looking as if he thought his last hour had come, and went to have a look at the van. He put out a great clawed foot, in a thoughtful sort of way, and tore the loose door off it. Then he tucked the door under his right front foreleg and departed, deliberately slowly, on three legs, helping himself with his wings, so that rocks rattled and flapped all along the valley.

Alectis sat down rather suddenly. But Lewin made him leap up again and help Terens get the broadcaster out of the van before any more dragons found it. They never did get it out. They were still working and waggling at it to get it loose, and Lewin was standing over Neal and me, so that we couldn't sneak off, when we heard that humming kind of whistle that you get from a dragon in flight. We whirled round. This dragon was a big black one, coasting low over the hill opposite and gliding down the valley. They don't often fly high. It came to ground with that grinding of stones and leathery slap of wings closing that always tells you a dragon is landing. It arched its black neck and looked at us disdainfully.

Orm was sitting on its back looking equally disdainful.

It was one of those times when Orm looks grave and grand. He sat very upright, with his hair and beard combed straight by the wind of flying, and his big pale eyes hardly looked mad at all. Neal was the only one of us he deigned to notice. "Good afternoon, Neal Sigridsson," he said. "You keep bad company. Dragonate are not human."

Neal was very angry with Orm. He put my heart in my mouth by saying, quite calmly, "Then in that case, I'm the only human here." With that dragon standing glaring! I've been brought up to despise boys, but I think that is a mistake.

To my relief, Orm just grinned. "That's the way, boy," he said. "Not a booby after all, are you?"

Then Lewin took my breath away by going right up to the dragon. He had his gun, of course, but that wouldn't have been much use against a dragon. He went so near that the dragon had to turn its head out of his way. "We've dropped the charges," he said. "And you should never have brought them."

Orm looked down at him. "You," he said, "know a thing or two."

"I know dragons don't willingly attack humans," Lewin said. "I always read up on a case before I hear it." At this, Orm put on his crazy look and made his mad cackle. "Stop that!" said Lewin. "The Slavers have invaded. Wormstow's full of Slaver troops and we need your help. I want to get everyone from the outlying farms into the Reserve and persuade the dragons to protect them. Can you help us do that?"

That took my breath away again, and Neal's too. We did a quick goggle at one another. Perhaps the Dragonate was like it was supposed to be after all!

Orm said, "Then we'd better get busy," and slid down from the dragon. He still towered over Lewin. Orm is huge. As soon as he was down, the black dragon lumbered across to the van and started taking it to bits. That brought other dragons coasting whistling in from all sides of the valley, to crunch to earth and hurry to the van too. In seconds, it was surrounded in black and green-brown shapes the size of haybarns. And Orm talked, at the top of his voice, through the sound of metal tearing, and big claws screaming on iron, and wings clapping, and angry grunts when two dragons happened to get hold of the same piece of van. Orm always talks a lot. But this time, he was being particularly garrulous, to give the dragons time to lumber away with their pieces of van, hide them and come back. "They won't even do what Orm says until they've got their metal," I whispered to Terens, who got rather impatient with Orm.

Orm said the best place to put people was the high valley at the center of the Reserve. "There's an old she-drake with a litter just hatched," he said. "No one will get past her when she's feared for her young. I'll speak to her. But the rest are to promise me she's not disturbed." As for telling everyone at the farms where to come, Orm said the dragons could do that, provided Lewin could think of a way of sending a message by them. "You see, most folk can't hear a dragon when it speaks," he said. "And some who can hear—" with a nasty look at me "—speak back to wound." He was still very angry with me. I kept on the other side of Terens and Alectis when the dragons all came swooping back.

Terens set the memo block to *repeat* and tapped out an official message from Lewin. Then he tore off page after page with the same thing on it. Orm handed each page to a dragon, saying things like, "Take this to the fat cow up at Hillfoot." Or, "Drop this on young vinegar lady at Crowtop—hard." Or, "This is for Dopey at High Jiot, but don't give it her, give it to her youngest husband or they'll never get moving."

Some of the things he said made me laugh a lot. But it was only when Alectis asked what was so funny and Neal kicked my ankle, that I realized I was the only one who could hear the things Orm said. Each dragon, as it got its page, ran down the valley and took off, showering us with stones from the jump they gave to get higher in the air than usual. Their wings boom when they fly high. Orm took off on the black dragon last of all, saying he would go and warn the she-drake.

Lewin crumpled his face ruefully at the few bits of van remaining, and we set off to walk to the valley ourselves. It was a long way. Over ling slopes and up among boulders in the kyle we trudged, looking up nervously every so often when fat bluish Slaver fliers screamed through the clouds overhead. After a while, our dragons began booming overhead too, seawards to roost. Terens counted them and said every one we had sent seemed to have come back now. He said he wished he had wings. It was sunset by the time we reached the valley. By that time,

Lewin was bent over, holding his chest and swearing every other step. But everyone was still pretending, in that stupid Dragonate way, that he was all right. We came up on the cliffs, where the kyle winds down to the she-drake's valley, and there was the sunset lighting the sea and the towers of rock out there, and the waves crashing round the rocks, where the young dragons were flying to roost—and Lewin actually pretended to admire the view. "I knew a place like this on Seven," he said. "Except there were trees instead of dragons. I can't get used to the way Eight doesn't have trees."

He was going to sit down to rest, I think, but Orm came up the kyle just then. Huffle was hulking behind him. "So you got here at last!" Orm said in his rudest way.

"We have," said Lewin. "Now would you mind telling me what you were playing at bringing those charges against Siglin?"

"You should be glad I did. You'd all be in a slaveship now if I hadn't," Orm said.

"But you weren't to know that, were you?" Terens said.

"Not to speak of risking being charged yourself," added Lewin.

Orm leant on his hand against Huffle, like you might against a wall. "She half killed this dragon!" he said. "That's why! All I did was ask her for a kiss and she screams and lays into poor Huffle. My own daughter, and she tries to kill a dragon! And I thought, Right, my lady, then you're no daughter of mine any more! And I flew Huffle's mother straight into Holmstad and laid charges. I was that angry! My own father tended dragons, and his mother before him. And my daughter tried to kill one! You wonder why I was angry?"

"Nobody *told* me!" I said. I had that draining-away feeling again. I was quite glad when Terens took hold of my elbow and said something like, "Steady, steady!"

"Are you telling the truth?" Neal said.

"I'm sure he is," Lewin said. "Your sister has his eyes."

"Ask Timas," said Orm. "He married your mother the year after I did. He can take being bossed about. I can't. I went back to my dragons. But I suppose there's a record of that?" he said challengingly to Lewin.

"And the divorce," said Lewin. "Terens looked it up for me. But I expect the Slavers have destroyed it by now."

"And she never told you?" Orm said to me. He wagged his shaggy eyebrows at me almost forgivingly. "I'll have a bone to pick with her over that," he said.

Mother arrived just as we'd all got down into the valley. She looked very indomitable, as she always does on horseback, and all our people were with her, down to both our shepherds. They had carts of clothes and blankets and food. Mother knew the valley as well as Orm did. She used to meet Orm there when she was a girl. She set out for the Reserve as soon as she heard the broadcast about the invasion, and the dragon we sent her met them on the way. That's Mother for you. The rest of the neighbors didn't get there for some hours after that.

I didn't think Mother's face—or Timas's—could hold such a mixture of feelings as they did when they saw Neal and me and the Dragonate men all with Orm. When Orm saw Mother, he folded his arms and grinned. Huffle rested his huge chin on Orm's shoulder, looking interested.

"Here she comes," Orm said to Huffle. "Oh, I do love a good quarrel!"

They had one. It was one of the loudest I'd ever heard. Terens took Neal and me away to help look after Lewin. He turned out to have broken some ribs when the blast hit the van, but he wouldn't let anyone look even until I ordered him to. After that, Neal, Alectis and I sat under our haycart and talked, mostly about the irony of Fate. You see, Neal has always secretly wished Fate had given him Orm as a father, and I'm the one that's got Orm. Neal's father is Timas. Alectis says he can see the likeness. We'd both gladly swap. Then Alectis confessed that he'd been hating the Dragonate so much that he was thinking of running away—which is a serious crime. But now the Slavers have come, and there doesn't seem to be much of a Dragonate any more, he feels quite different. He admires Lewin.

Lewin consented to rest while Terens and Mother organized everyone into a makeshift camp in the valley, but he was up and about again the next day, because he said the Slavers were bound to come the day after, when they found the holdings were deserted. The big black she-drake sat in her cave at the head of the kyle, with her infants between her forefeet, watching groups of people rushing round to do what Lewin said, and didn't seem to mind at all. Huffle said she'd been bored and bad-tempered up to then. We made life interesting. Actually that she-drake reminds me of Mother. Both of them made me give them a faithful report of the battle.

I don't think the Slavers knew about the dragons. They

just knew that there was a concentration of people in here, and they came straight across the Reserve to get us. As soon as the dragons told Orm they were coming, Lewin had us all out hiding in the hills in their path, except for Mother and Timas and Inga's mother and a few more who had shotguns. They had to stay and guard the little kids in the camp. The rest of us had any weapon we could find. Neal and Alectis had bows and arrows. Inga had her air-gun. Donal and most of the farmers had scythes. The shepherds all had their slingshots. I was in the front with Lewin, because I was supposed to stop the effect of the Slavers' collars. Orm was there too, although nobody had ever admitted in so many words that Orm might be heg. All Orm did was to ask the dragons to keep back, because we didn't want *them* enslaved by those collars.

And there they came, a huddle of sheep-like troops, and then another huddle, each one being driven by a cluster of kingly Slavers, with crowns and winking V-shaped collars. And there again we all got that horrible guilty compulsion to come and give ourselves up. But I don't think those collars have any effect on dragons. Half of us were standing up to walk into the Slavers' arms, and I was ordering them as hard as I could not to, when the dragons smelt those golden crowns and collars. There was no holding them. They just whirred down over our heads and took those Slavers to pieces for the metal. Lewin said, "Ah!" and crumpled his face in a grin like a fiend's. He'd thought the dragons might do that. I think he may really be a genius, like they say Camerati are. But I was so sick at that, and then again at the sight of nice people like Alectis and Yan killing the sheep-like troops, that I'm not going to talk about it any more. Terens says I'm not to go when the Slavers come next. Apparently I broadcast the way I was feeling, just like the Slavers do, and even the dragons felt queasy. The she-drake snorted at that. Mother says, "Nonsense. Take travel pills and behave as my daughter should."

Anyway, we have found out how to beat the Slavers. We have no idea what is going on in the other of the Ten Worlds, or even in the rest of Sveridge, but there are fifty more Worm Reserves around the world, and Lewin says there must be stray Dragonate units too who might think of using dragons against Slavers. We want to move out and take over some of the farms again soon. The dragons are having far too much fun with the sheep. They keep flying over with woolly bundles dangling from their claws, watched by a gloomy crowd of everyone's shepherds. "Green dot," the shepherds say. "The brutes are raiding Hightop now." They are very annoyed with Orm, because Orm just gives his mad cackle and lets the dragons go on.

Orm isn't mad at all. He's afraid of people knowing he's heg—he still won't admit he is. I think that's why he left Mother and Mother doesn't admit she was ever married to him. Not that Mother minds. I get the feeling she and Orm understand one another rather well. But Mother married Donal, you see, after Timas. Donal, and Yan too, have both told me that the fact that I'm heg makes no difference to them—but you should see the way they both look at me! I'm not fooled. I don't blame Orm for being scared stiff Donal would find out he was heg. But I'm not sure I shall ever like Orm, all the same.

I am putting all this down on what is left of Palino's memo block. Lewin wanted me to, in case there is still some History yet to come. He has made his official version on the recorder. I'm leaning the block on Huffle's forefoot. Huffle is my friend now. Leaning on a dragon is the best way to keep warm on a chilly evening like this, when you're forced to camp out in the Reserve. Huffle is letting Lewin lean on him too, beyond Neal, because Lewin's ribs still pain him. There is a lot of leaning-space along the side of a dragon. Orm has just stepped across Huffle's tail, into the light, chortling and rubbing his hands in his most irritating way.

"Your mother's on the warpath," he says. "Oh, I do love a good quarrel!"

And here comes Mother, ominously upright, and with her arms folded. It's not Orm she wants. It's Lewin. "Listen, you," she says. "What the dickens is the Dragonate thinking of, beheading hegs all these years? They can't help what they are. And they're the only people who can stand up to the Thrallers."

Orm is cheated of his quarrel. Lewin looked up, crumpled into the most friendly smile. "I do so agree with you," he said. "I've just said so in my report. And I'd have got your daughter off somehow, you know."

Orm is cackling like the she-drake's young ones. Mother's mouth is open and I really think that, for once in her life, she has no idea what to say.

Buried Treasure

by Tim Waggoner

It was Thanksgiving Day—leaves down, trees bare, air cold and clear—when Nina and I found the spaceship.

Dinner was over, and we were both bored. Every year, our families got together in the afternoon to watch football on TV, but neither of us liked sitting around; we'd rather go outside and do something. So while everyone else digested turkey in front of the tube, Nina and I headed for the woods behind her house.

"Let's hunt for pirate treasure," Nina said as she crunched through a pile of dry red and gold leaves.

"In the woods?" I asked. "In Ohio? Give me a break, Neen."

She grinned. "Maybe they wanted to make *really* sure no other pirates could find it."

"Considering the nearest ocean is hundreds of miles away, I'd say they picked a good place."

I was twelve and a half; Nina was thirteen. She said this was proof positive that girls mature faster than boys, and she never missed an opportunity to remind me of this "fact."

"Maybe you're right," she said thoughtfully. "Pirates is kind of a baby game. How about we play tag instead?"

Nina whirled around and before I could react, she slammed her palms against my chest and shoved. Caught off guard, I fell backward and landed hard on my rear, the air whooshing out of my lungs.

"You're it!" Nina shouted gleefully and dashed off.

I got to my feet and gave pursuit, half running and half hobbling as I struggled to catch my breath. I recovered quickly, and soon we were both running full speed, weaving around tree trunks, going farther and farther into the woods, deeper than we'd ever been before. Nina's laughter floated behind her, challenging me to run harder, faster. Part of me was afraid of getting lost. The town we lived in, Dryden, sat on the edge of a state park, and Nina's house bordered the largest, wildest part of that park. The woods were huge; what if we couldn't find our way back?

But then Nina would laugh again, and I'd forget my misgivings and redouble my efforts to catch her.

Eventually, I closed the distance between us, and I reached out for Nina's jacket, intending to grab it and force her to stop. My fingers brushed the cloth, but before I could get a grip, Nina suddenly stumbled forward with cry of alarm and hit the ground. It was all I could do to keep from running over her.

I stopped and leaned over to catch my breath. "Are . . . you . . . okay?" I wheezed.

Nina sat up with a groan and cradled her right leg. Her pants were torn over the knee, and I could see blood dotted with bits of leaf and twig. She inspected her wound, barely breathing hard. She'd always been more athletic than I.

"It stings, but I think I'll live."

I held out a hand to her. "Why don't you see if you can stand on it?"

She nodded and I helped her up. She winced when she put weight on her injured leg, but after a few tentative steps, she was walking normally again.

I reached out and touched her lightly on the shoulder. "By the way, tag."

She gave me a sour look. "Very funny." She knelt down and began rummaging through the leaves.

"Drop something?" I asked.

"I'm trying to find whatever it was that I tripped—" She broke off, drawing her hand away from the ground with a sudden violent motion, as if she'd been bitten by a snake.

At first, that's exactly what I feared had happened, though I doubted any snakes would be slithering about as cold as it was. But before I could express my concern, Nina said, "Don't worry, I'm all right. I just touched something that felt really weird." Frowning, she reached back down and carefully brushed leaves away from the whatever-it-was.

Intrigued, I knelt to help her. We finished clearing the leaves to reveal a mound of earth about twice the size of a softball. Some of the dirt had been knocked away, probably when Nina's foot hit it, and a patch of silver shone through.

She pointed toward the metallic-looking substance. "That's what I touched. It was cold, like ice, and it . . . tingled."

Nina had an overactive imagination, so when I reached down to touch the silver material, I didn't expect to feel much of anything. But as soon as my skin came in contact with the metal, I yanked my hand away.

"That's really freaky. It feels like it's vibrating."

"Maybe it's some kind of machine." She moved to touch it again, but I grabbed her wrist to stop her.

"It could be dangerous," I warned. "A power line or something."

She gave me a look that said I was the biggest moron on the planet. "It doesn't look like a power line. And neither of us got shocked when we touched it before." She pulled her hand free and then pressed her index finger against the metal. Her arm jerked once, probably a reflex, but she didn't draw back this time.

Minutes passed, and Nina got a faraway look in her eyes, as if she were thinking about something important and puzzling.

"What is it?" I asked. I wanted to know what was on her mind, but she misunderstood.

"I don't know what it is." She grinned. "Why don't we dig it up and see?"

"Well, Pirate Nina, whatever it is, it's not buried treasure."

We'd worked for over an hour, jabbing and overturning earth with broken tree limbs and scraping dirt with our bare—and now filthy—hands and nails. We'd managed to expose several feet of the silver stuff. It was all bumps (like the one Nina had tripped over) and curlicued lines which were etched into the metal.

"I don't know about that," she said as she slowly traced one of the lines with her fingers. "It's strange; the smooth parts of the metal are freezing cold, but these lines are warm, almost hot in some places. And I think I can hear a soft buzzing sound."

I listened, but I didn't hear anything, and I told Nina so. She shrugged. "Like I said, it's real soft." She stood, but she didn't take her eyes off the thing we'd found.

"You know what, Austin? I think we've found a UFO."

I started to laugh, wanted to tell her she was crazy, that her imagination had gone too far this time. But standing in the thick of the woods, looking at the strange bumps and swirling patterns which covered the metal, I almost believed her.

I glanced up at sky. "We've got to go, Nina. It's getting late. It'll probably be dark before we get home." *If we can find our way back,* I added mentally.

Nina didn't respond, and I had to grip her elbow and pull her away from our discovery.

"Okay, okay, I'm coming," she snapped. But as we walked, she kept glancing back at our find, the expression on her face unreadable.

"If it is a UFO, where did it come from?"

"From space, dummy," Nina said witheringly.

"No, I mean how did it get buried in the ground?"

"I don't know," she said. "Maybe it crashed a million years ago. Maybe it was a probe that got left behind when its builders were done with it. It doesn't really matter how it got there, does it? Just so long as it's *there.*"

It was Friday morning, and Nina had called and invited me to go for a walk in the woods. I biked over, but before heading out, we stopped in the garage and picked up some tools.

Now we were walking among the trees, me carrying a

pick-ax, Nina a shovel. I was afraid we might not be able to locate the place again—we'd had a hard enough time finding our way back home yesterday—but Nina walked with unerring confidence, as if she had a compass in her head.

We walked in silence for a time before Nina spoke again. "I had some really weird dreams last night."

"Yeah? How weird?"

"I don't know. Weird. I was flying, I think. I remember clouds and wind. It was like I could see all around me, you know, the way a fly does? And I could see more than just the sky—I saw all sorts of colors . . . colors I don't have any names for, maybe which nobody has any names for."

She broke off, clearly embarrassed. We walked along in silence a bit more before I finally said, "You're right: that's pretty weird."

She slugged me on the shoulder, not hard, and we continued on. We found the silver metal easily, and without speaking, we started to dig. It wasn't like on TV and in the movies, where people start to dig and then there's a switch to the next scene and they're all done (and barely sweaty). It was hard work. The soil was more like rock than dirt, and before long my arms and back were aching and I was breathing heavily. Nina didn't seem to be as affected by her exertions, though I noticed she slowed down after a bit.

At one point, tired, hot, and covered with sweat, I swung the pick and instead of it thunking into the earth, it clanged onto the metal.

Nina let out a screech, as if I'd accidentally killed a puppy or something. She dropped her shovel and rushed over to check out the damage I'd done, but the metal wasn't even scratched. She breathed a sigh of relief, shot me a warning look to tell me to be more careful, and we both resumed digging.

Finally, too tired and sore to continue, I called it quits. Nina looked like she could go on digging for another couple hours, but she stopped too. All our work, and we'd only exposed a few more square feet of the spaceship, and what we'd uncovered didn't look any different, just more raised bumps and curvey, swirling lines.

I was surprised to find myself disappointed. I'd been half hoping to find a door or a window. Something that would prove this really was—or wasn't—a spaceship.

Nina didn't seemed bothered by our less-than-spectacular results. She knelt next to the exposed metal and placed her palms on its bumpy surface. This time, she didn't draw back when her flesh made contact with the silvery surface.

"It feels different today," she said in a dreamy voice. "Warmer, not so tingly. I—"

She didn't finish. As I watched, her hands began to slowly sink into the surface of the strange object we'd discovered, as if it were now made of thick silver goo instead of metal.

"Nina!" I shouted. "Get away from it!"

But if she heard me, she didn't listen. She closed her eyes and started humming. Her hands continued sinking, faster now, wrists gone, forearms disappearing, silver sliding toward elbows. Terrified, I ran over, wrapped my arms around her waist, and pulled. Nothing happened at first; it was as if her arms were imbedded in concrete. I pulled harder, gritting my teeth, determined not to lose my friend to whatever horrible thing we'd found. Finally, I felt her give a little and I put all of my strength into one last backward pull, and with an awful sucking sound, Nina's arms came free.

We fell backward in heap and lay on the forest floor for a moment. I felt like crying out of both fear and relief, but I didn't. I didn't want Nina to see me cry, didn't want her to know how scared I'd been. Didn't want her to know how much she meant to me.

I glanced at the metal. The surface was solid and unbroken once more, with no sign of where Nina's hands had sunk into it.

After a moment, she pulled free of my embrace—I was still holding her without realizing it—and stood.

"Why did you do that?" she said, half accusation, half sob. "Why?"

She looked down at me, tears running from the corners of her eyes.

It may have been a trick of the light, but for a second it looked as if she were crying tears of silver.

She touched the thing again, despite my protests, but nothing happened this time. We gathered our tools and headed back to Nina's house. She didn't talk to me the whole way. I could tell she was pretty mad, but I didn't care. She was okay, and that was all that mattered to me.

I went home and later that night, after supper, I gave her a call.

"We never should have dug that thing up," I said. "Whatever it is, it's way too dangerous."

"It's not dangerous."

"It almost ate you today!"

She laughed softly. "It didn't try to eat me, stupid. It was trying to let me in. It doesn't have doors like we think of them."

"How do you know so much about it all of a sudden?"

"Because when it tried to let me inside we . . . connected. I knew what it was thinking, what it was feeling."

"You mean it's *alive*?"

"Not exactly, not in the way you mean," she said. "But it has a mind. It's lonely, Austin. It's been in the ground for a very long time."

"You're starting to scare me, Nina. Please tell me you're putting me on."

"I'm serious. We were right; it is a spaceship, but instead of flying it like an airplane, the pilot *joins* with it. Becomes part of the ship. But this one's pilot grew old and sick. They searched for someone to take the pilot's place, but he died before they could find anyone. Without a pilot, the ship was unable to fly on its own, and it crashlanded on Earth. I don't know how long ago, maybe even before the dinosaurs. It's been buried all this time, until we found it."

The calm certainty in Nina's voice convinced me she was telling the truth. At least, the truth as she believed it.

"The ship is so sad, Austin. It's been caught in the earth for millions of years, when it should be free, soaring among the stars."

"We should tell someone. Our parents, or maybe one of the teachers at school."

"We can't do that! If the government finds out about the ship, they'll want to cut it into pieces and study it. They'll kill it, Austin! We can't let that happen!"

I didn't believe the ship—if it really was a ship—was alive, but I didn't want to upset Nina further. "Then we'll cover it back up so no one else can find it. It'll be safe that way."

Nina didn't say anything. I knew what she was thinking. She's always been the more adventurous of the two of us, more impulsive, more willing to take chances.

"Promise me you'll stay away from it, Neen. Tomorrow we'll go there and bury it again, and it'll all be over. Okay?" I waited for her to answer, and when she didn't, repeated, more strongly, "Okay?"

So softly I almost couldn't hear her, she whispered, "I promise," and then hung up without saying good-bye.

I didn't sleep well that night. I tossed and turned mostly, and when I did sleep, I dreamed that I was digging an endless pit, going deeper and deeper, until the walls caved in on me, and I couldn't move, couldn't breathe.

The first thing I did the next morning was call Nina's house.

Her mother answered, and she was surprised when I asked for Nina.

"She told me she was going over to your house. She left a half hour ago."

"I'm sorry, I just got out of bed and I'm not thinking too clearly yet. Nina's probably downstairs watching TV or something, waiting for me." I hung up before Nina's mom could question my weak story. I dressed quickly and rushed out the door without telling my own parents where I was going. I hopped on my bike and pedaled as hard and fast as I could toward Nina's.

I wasn't sure I could find my way back to the spot without Nina's guidance, but whether through instinct or blind luck, I did. I shouted Nina's name as I approached, but there was no answer.

I reached the part of the woods where we had uncovered the ship. But instead of a silver mound, there was a depression of crumbled, broken earth. Fear lanced through my gut. The ship had taken off! But then I realized it couldn't have; something as large as a spaceship would have ripped up the ground a lot more than this, I reasoned, maybe even left behind some burn marks, like from rocket exhaust. But then what had caused—

Austin . . .

Nina's voice, little more than a whisper. But I hadn't heard it, at least not with my ears. It came from inside my head.

Look up. Her "voice" sounded amused this time.

I did as she told me and there, hovering above the trees, bright silver against the blue of the sky, was the ship. It was big, though its exact size was hard to judge because it kept shifting its shape. First it was round, then triangular; an oval, then a rectangle, and then a series of shapes which I didn't recognize. Its surface changed textures too. Sometimes it was covered with bumps and lines, other times it was smooth, and sometimes it rippled as if it were made out of liquid.

I understood then how it had gotten out of the ground without making more of a mess. Once Nina was inside and the ship had a pilot again, it was able to change its shape and flow out of the hole we had made, leaving the earth to collapse in upon the empty space where it had rested for millions of years.

I spoke, knowing somehow that Nina would be able to hear me. "Are . . . are you okay?"

I'm better than okay, Austin. I'm fabulous! The ship flashed into the shape of a silver starburst, mirroring Nina's enthusiasm. *You can't imagine what it's like. There are no words to describe it!*

I knew she was talking about being joined to the ship. Was she hooked up to it by cables and wires, or had the alien technology merged with her in ways I couldn't imagine? I didn't want to think about it.

"Nina, please, come down."

Her laughter echoed through my mind. *Are you kidding? This is the chance of a lifetime! Of a zillion-zillion lifetimes! I'm going to see the galaxy, Austin! I'm going to see everything!*

"What about your mom and dad, Neen?"

She was silent for a few moments, and the ship remained in a single shape for a time.

Tell Mom and Dad I love them, but I have to go. The ship needs me, Austin. And I need it.

"What about . . . me?"

A bulge formed on the underside of the ship and a silver tentacle extruded. It coiled down toward me, two handles forming on its side as it lowered.

Come with us, Austin. We'll sail away together and be pirates of the universe. Just think of all the treasures we'll find!

I was tempted. I went so far as to reach out for the tendril-ladder Nina had provided for me. But in the end I couldn't do it. I was too afraid of leaving everyone and everything I knew behind for whatever unknown adventures Nina and the ship promised.

"I'm sorry," I said as I withdrew my hands.

I understand, Nina thought, though I could sense her disappointment. *You take care of yourself, Austin.*

The ship flowed into a teardrop shape—whether because it needed to in order to depart or because it was mirroring Nina's sadness, I don't know—and a powerful hum began to build. I knew Nina and the ship were preparing to leave.

I cupped my hands to my mouth and shouted to be heard above the noise. "Come back and visit sometime!"

Space is awfully big, and Time doesn't always run the way you want it to, but I'll try. Good-bye, Austin.

And then the ship shot straight up, so fast that I couldn't see it go. One moment it was there, the next gone, and I was being buffeted by the winds stirred up in its wake. After the winds died down, I watched the sky for a long time and wondered if I'd made the right decision.

*   *   *

I told Nina's parents what happened, but of course they didn't believe me. They thought she ran away. After a while, I started to think that maybe they were right, that the spaceship had just been a figment of my imagination, something my mind invented to cope with Nina's leaving.

But last night I had a dream. Nina and the ship were heading for Earth. They were coming home.

That's why I'm sitting out here in the woods and writing all this down in a notebook, so whoever finds it will know what happened to me. Please give it to my parents. Their address and phone number are written on the inside front cover.

As Nina said, it's a chance in a lifetime. A zillion-zillion lifetimes.

Mom, Dad—assuming you ever see this—please show it to Nina's parents and tell them they have nothing to worry about. Nina's just fine.

We both are.

ABOUT THE AUTHORS

NOREEN DOYLE belongs to several Egyptological organizations and is an expert on ancient Egyptian watercraft. Her stories have appeared in *Realms of Fantasy*, *Weird Tales*, *Century*, and *Bruce Coville's Strange Worlds*.

HARLAN ELLISON has been called "one of the greatest living American short story writers" by *The Washington Post*. His many accomplishments include winning the Hugo Award eight and a half times, and the Edgar Award of the Mystery Writers of America twice. Among his most recognized works are the short story anthologies *Deathbird Stories*, *Strange Wine*, *I Have No Mouth & I Must Scream*, *Ellison Wonderland*, and *Shatterday*. He lives in Los Angeles, California.

DAVID HONIGSBERG lives, works, and writes in New York City. His short stories have appeared in numerous anthologies, including *Elric: Tales of the White Wolf* and *On Crusade: More Tales of the Knights Templar*. A guitarist and songwriter, he is also a founding member of the Don't Quit Your Day Job Players.

GREG LaBARBERA lives in Charlotte, North Carolina, with his wife, Jackie, and their three black Labradors. Besides writing stories for young people, Greg enjoys writing songs and playing guitar in his rock band Small Time Joe. His short story "Jonas. Just Jonas"—written with Nancy Varian Berberick—appeared in *Bruce Coville's Shapeshifters*. Of the many places Greg gets his story ideas, the thought of a big ball crushing a small town came from his good friend, Ken Gunn.

JOHN MORRESSY is the author of a couple of dozen novels, and many short stories that have appeared in *Science and Science Fiction*, *Asimov's*, *Esquire*, and *Omni*. His latest novel, *The Juggler*, is a young adult historical fantasy. John lives in New Hampshire with his wife and cat, and plans to write a great many more Kedrigern stories.

GORDON LINZNER is a native New Yorker. He has published three novels and some two dozen short stories—mostly fantasy and horror—and has been editor/publisher of *Space and Time* magazine since 1966. "Field Trip" is his first science fiction sale.

NICHOLAS FISK is the author of over two dozen science-fiction short stories and books. Among his novels are *Mindbenders*, *A Hole in the Head*, and *Grinny*. His novel *Monster Maker* was made into a film by Henson Associates. His short story "Whooo-ooo, Flupper!" appeared in *Bruce Coville's Strange Worlds*.

NANCY ETCHEMENDY has been writing books and stories since fifth grade, though she's only been publishing them since 1980. Her story "Bigger Than Death" won the 1998 Bram Stoker Award for dark fiction in a work for young readers. Before she wrote "Fireflies," she liked peanut butter a lot.

AL SARRANTONIO is the author of twenty novels in the science fiction, horror, mystery, and Western genres, including the critically acclaimed *Five Worlds* trilogy. He has been nominated for the Horror Writers Association's Bram Stoker Award as well as for the Shamus Award of the Private Eye Writers of America.

MICHAEL MARKIEWICZ's stories have appeared in several Bruce Coville anthologies. He is a regular speaker at schools and libraries, where his "Arthur and Cai" stories are very popular. Michael lives in rural Pennsylvania with his wife, Lois, his son, Christopher, and their two "totally spastic" beagles, Nick and Pen.

MARK A. GARLAND has spent the last dozen years reading, going back to school, attending conventions, and writing. His works include *Dinotopia* and *Star Trek* books, as well as his original novel *Sword of the Prophets*, and nearly fifty published poems, articles, and short stories; one story was published in *Bruce Coville's Shapeshifters*. Mark lives in upstate New York with his wife, their three children, and (of course) a cat.

DIANA WYNNE JONES is one of the UK's best-known writers of children's fantasy. Since 1973, she has written over thirty novels and stories, ranging from fantasy to science fiction, for children and for adults, from dark to humorous; among her most famous works are the *Dalemark Series* and the *Chrestomanci Series*. In 1999, she won the Mythopoeic Award for children's fantasy literature and the Karl Edward Wagner Award, given by the British Fantasy Society to individuals who have made a significant impact on the genre. Her latest book, *Believing is Seeing*, was published in 1999 by Greenwillow Books.

TIM WAGGONER's other stories for young readers have appeared in *Bruce Coville's Book of Nightmares 2* and the forthcoming *Half Human*. All in all, he's published around fifty tales of fantasy and horror. He teaches creative writing at Sinclair Community College in Dayton, Ohio.

About the Artists

ERNIE COLÓN, cover and interior artist, has worked on a wide variety of comic book-related projects during the course of his long career, including graphic novels, comic strips, and various superhero titles. His most current work came in providing the cover paintings for *Bruce Coville's Alien Visitors*, *Bruce Coville's Shapeshifters*, and *Bruce Coville's Strange Worlds*; he also pencilled the interior art for the latter two. Ernie lives on Long Island, New York, with his wife and daughter.

JOHN NYBERG, who inked the story illustrations, has been a comic book artist for fourteen years. Among his many accomplishments are *Green Arrow*, *Plastic Man*, and *The Flash* for DC Comics; *Doom 2099* for Marvel; and *WildC.A.T.S.* and *Gen^{13}* for Image. His most recent work was as inker for *Bruce Coville's Alien Visitors* and *Bruce Coville's Shapeshifters*. John lives in New Jersey with his wife, Amy, and their two cats, Bart and Lisa.

BRUCE COVILLE was born in Syracuse, New York, and grew up in a rural area north of the city, around the corner from his grandparents' dairy farm. He lives in a brick house in Syracuse with his wife, his youngest child, four cats, and a jet-propelled Norwegian elk hound named Thor. Though he has been a teacher, a toymaker, and a gravedigger, he prefers writing. His dozens of books for young readers include the bestselling *My Teacher Is an Alien* series, *Goblins in the Castle*, *Aliens Ate My Homework*, and *Sarah's Unicorn*. His most recent work is the book and television series *I Was a Sixth Grade Alien*.